# PRAISE FOR
# THE CLANDESTINE CONSULTANT

*"Luke Bencie's "The Clandestine Consultant" offers a realistic glimpse into the world of US intelligence and the shadowy regions of the world where its operatives and cohorts orbit one another. Though a work of fiction, this book should be considered a prime resource for anyone seeking a better understanding of modern spycraft. It provides rich insight into the global intelligence apparatus, which today is populated by actors from both governments and the private sector, and melds the two into a compelling storyline. Readers will walk away with a better understanding of the world in which we all live.*

**-General James L. Jones (Retired), Former US National Security Advisor**

*"Bencie's book provides the reader with a unique and tantalizing look into the mysterious world of high-level, top secret intelligence consultants. The situation in the world today, provides a backdrop for the events that take place in the book and makes its relevance even more meaningful."*

**-William Esposito, Former FBI Deputy Director**

*"A great spy thriller with surprising twists upon twists and hair raising excitements -- the hero, a businessman spy, plies his trade around the globe in some of the most volatile areas in today's news . . . the tale is chock full of real spy tradecraft and cleverly drawn shady and dangerous characters"*

**-Mike Sulick, Former Director of the CIA's National Clandestine Service**

*"Most people cannot even comprehend that nefarious people like this actually exist... after three decades of bringing these characters to justice, believe me they do."*

**-Malcolm Brady, Former Assistant Director of the Bureau of Alcohol, Tobacco, and Firearms**

*"A fascinating thriller that keeps you spell-bound, make sure you don't miss the real-life lessons and advice on personal security"*

**-Lt. General PT Mikolashek (Retired), Former Inspector General, US Army and Commanding General, Third United States Army**

*"A gripping account of [fictional reality]". . . "a daunting repertoire of [if, when] scenarios haunting the mind of every consultant working on the global stage."*

**-Steven H. Gurley, Former FBI, Special Agent In Charge and former Deputy Director of CIA's Counterterrorist Center**

*"Most business leaders, wise in the way of the balance sheet and masterful in the art of the deal, are surprisingly naive about the wiles of global trouble spots, which is why they need to read 'The Clandestine Consultant'."*

**-François Baird, Chairman, Baird's CMC, an international firm of communications management consultants in 17 countries**

"A must read for the business leader who travels the world! While fictional in content, Bencie's real-world experiences blended into this book provides the reader an intriguing and insightful spy thriller. It shows the challenges, and unique 'characters,' the intelligence consultant must deal with in their day-to-day efforts. Reader take notice."

**-Maj. Gen. Edward A. Leacock, (Retired), Former Mobilization Assistant to the Director, Defense Intelligence Agency**

"Luke Bencie demonstrated his literary flair in Among Enemies: Counter-Espionage for the Business Traveler, a valuable guidebook on thwarting business travel espionage that rang true as the Liberty Bell - before it was cracked, that is. Its veracity stemmed from Bencie's own personal experiences across every continent on the earth. Most of those experiences were, of course, redacted by one government agency or another, which makes a novel the next logical step forward for Luke's storytelling. Nothing you read in spy novels or see in spy movies will prepare you for Bencie's first novel, The Clandestine Consultant. It's everything he couldn't write about in a nonfiction book, and he writes well. You will find yourself sucked down the international intrigue and danger rabbit hole, right behind The Tall Man. Move over, Alex Berenson. You've got competition."

**-Jack B. Rochester, Author of the Nathaniel Hawthorne Flowers novels: *Wild Blue Yonder - Madrone - Anarchy***

*The Clandestine Consultant*
by Luke Bencie

© Copyright 2017 Luke Bencie

ISBN 978-1-63393-419-1

Published by

◣ köehlerbooks ™

210 60th Street
Virginia Beach, VA 23451
800-435-4811
www.koehlerbooks.com

# THE
# CLANDESTINE

KINGS, SHEIKS, WARLORDS, AND DICTATORS

# CONSULTANT

## LUKE BENCIE

*For Mick*

*"In the midst of chaos, there is also opportunity."*
-Sun Tzu, from *The Art of War*

# PROLOGUE

*Location:* *Somewhere within the Federally Administered Tribal Areas (FATA), along the Afghanistan-Pakistan border*
*Time:* *Unknown*

I open my eyes and can't see. I am having trouble breathing. The air is rancid and stale. I hear yelling but I can't understand any of it. I can't move. My arms are tied behind my back, my feet are bound and I am lying on my side. Pain erupts in the side of my head. I think the butt of a rifle has just struck me in the temple. Vomit covers my face. I realize that there must be some type of sack over my head.

Immediately, a bright white light burns my eyes, as the sack is ripped off. I put my forehead to the ground to shield my eyes. The yelling persists. Another pain shoots through my ribs from a boot planted in my side. The acrid, rusty taste of blood now replaces the residual vomit in my mouth. I am severely dehydrated and my brain is throbbing. I am confused and disoriented.

I try to regain my composure and look up at the men in front of me. There are three of them. Whalid Talibani, the imposing tribal warlord, stands in the middle. His two accomplices are wearing black hoods, their eyes glaring through makeshift holes cut in the fabric. They each hold AK-47s, while the hulking figure of Talibani swings a long machete-like knife like a pendulum. Still failing to grasp the complete picture of my surroundings, I look down upon my tired body kneeling in the dirt. Suddenly, a wave of fear jolts my senses into hyperdrive. My adrenaline is pumping at maximum capacity and my mind becomes more alert than a person high on cocaine for the first time. I piss myself without care. I have just realized that I am wearing a bright orange jumpsuit, the kind of standard-issue garment worn by terrorist detainees in prison camps or more importantly, the kind of jumpsuit worn by so-called "Western infidels" right before radical Islamists execute them on camera.

*This is it*, I think. *All my life's work, everything that I did up until this point, everyone I've ever met, this is how it ends.* I actually laugh at the thought of my next high school reunion, where all anyone there will talk about is how the guy they went to school with got his head chopped off on YouTube. But if that comes to pass, no one will ever know why; that's because no one knows who I am and what I do. That was apparent six weeks earlier on a flight from Dubai to Washington. It was the beginning of a journey that got me into this mess.

**Six weeks earlier . . .**

# IDENTITY

**Location:** *38,000 feet above the Atlantic Ocean on Emirates Air Flight 231 from Dubai to Washington, Seat 1A*
**Time:** *1200 hours*

To the other passengers sitting around me in first class, as well as the attentive cabin crew refilling my glass of Bordeaux, I was just another anonymous businessman somewhere between thirty-five and forty-five.

Little did they know I hold a treasure trove of interesting secrets—some of which have shaped the course of world history. In the very near future, more of these secrets will unfold into events with life-changing consequences for thousands of people. You might read about them in newspapers and wonder how or why they happened. Or, perhaps you won't hear of them at all. But I knew they were coming. I might even have caused them.

Who am I? Perhaps a spy, you might think. Maybe an assassin? More innocently, I might be lawyer, a lobbyist, or a diplomat. Or could it be that I'm a thief? What about an international arms dealer?

The truth is I am (in my mind, at least) none of these things. But by technical definition I am also all of them. But for now, call me an *international consultant*. That's what my business card reads, that and my email address: consultant@globalconsultant. com. Nothing more. Nothing less. Not even a name or phone number. My job is to advise and assist those at the highest levels of power and influence. My client list includes kings, sheiks, warlords, and dictators. Sometimes, I also help the ultra-rich and maybe the occasional high-level politician. I solve their toughest and most embarrassing problems. Discretion is my policy, and I am particular for whom I do work. That's why I avoid celebrities altogether. They're too emotionally unstable and cannot keep secrets.

As secretive and mysterious as I am, turn on the television and chances are you'll see the results of my work. At any given time, 75 percent of the planet is undergoing some form of turmoil or strife. Wars, uprisings, invasions, economic crises, insurrections, famine, disease—the list goes on and on. The world is not a nice place. Never has been. But where most people read the newspapers or their websites and bemoan the chaos and despair, I read them to scout for clients and profits. Single-paragraph news stories, tucked away in the bottom corner of the international section, provide me with an abundance of leads. You could say I specialize in the disreputable.

I don't advertise my services, nor do I solicit business from strangers. I work strictly by referrals from previous clients, some of whom, interestingly enough, despise one another so much they have tried killing one another. Remember the saying, "Keep your friends close and your enemies closer?" Well, I'm the person who maintains that relationship between enemies. I'm the ultimate middleman—a *fixer*.

Say your country needs to pass a message to another country with who you're at war. I'll be the conduit. Say you need to conduct a coup d'état in Africa. Be sure to call me first. I've compiled a solid track record of removing one political party and installing another. Want to host the World Cup in your country? I'm your best chance of discreetly negotiating the bribe to soccer officials on your behalf while keeping your reputation intact. Need to target the world's most-wanted criminals or terrorists? I'll point you in the right direction. Need to disappear? I have skills that would make Houdini blush. I *facilitate* and *eliminate*.

My services don't come cheap.

My bank accounts—scattered across several continents in various currencies—total around 40 million euros. The amount should be much higher, but I have a tendency to piss away money as quickly as I earn it. It's a decent sum for someone who grew up fairly modestly in a simple place, which is about the only hint of my past I'll share.

My name isn't important, either. Hell, I can't remember the last time someone actually called me by my birth name. Most of my clients simply refer to me as "The Tall Man," because I stand six-feet-four-inches, or nearly two meters. I enjoy being tall, but it can sometimes be an impediment to being clandestine. My nationality is equally unimportant. I have numerous names and passports—all genuine, I might add. I'm a distinguished gentleman, I speak five languages fluently and idiomatically, and my country-of-origin accent is virtually indistinguishable. My home is whatever five-star hotel room—or third-world hut—I might be staying in at the moment. I have no friends, unless you include the smiling faces of maître d's at the Michelin star-rated restaurants I frequent. I'm sure my tailors in Milan and New York would claim to be my friends; given the money I've spent with them over the years. My "significant others" consist of a series of exotic women living around the globe whom I might see a few times per year, if that. I am, as you can see, private and alone—and I prefer it that way.

Why do I do this type of work? Simple, I'm excellent at it. It keeps me challenged. I can't imagine holding an ordinary job. A banker? Please! A lawyer? Boring. A secret agent? Too much bureaucracy. In fact, most intelligence professionals will tell you that they sign up to be James Bond, but in truth spend more time behind a desk than Miss Moneypenny. In my world, I'm utterly free of the constraints that have been placed upon the masses—even the covert masses. Yet my existence, unpleasant as it might be to contemplate, is inevitable. I'm nothing new. People like me have operated through the centuries. You could even say we're necessary for society's evolution.

Please don't misunderstand me, however. I'm no Machiavelli. The 16th-century political realist and author of *The Prince* was more about his own personal notoriety and ascension up society's ladder—though there's no denying that some of Machiavelli's beliefs about elections are as prophetic today as they were 500 years ago. My favorite quote of his:

"Men are so naïve, and so much dominated by immediate

needs, that a skilful [sic] deceiver always finds plenty of people who let themselves be deceived."

In other words, as my father used to say, "The masses are asses."

I'm not a political campaign manager, either. Those guys are nothing more than modern-day charlatans. Instead, think of me as Telemus, the character from Greek mythology—the tiny man in Homer's *Odyssey* who whispered instructions into the ear of the mighty Cyclops, after Cyclops was blinded. I, too, whisper advice into the most misunderstood and challenged world leaders.

At this point you might be thinking I'm full of it. I must be some delusional fool living in a world of fanciful storytelling. My friend, that's exactly what I want you and everyone else to believe. But the truth is, men like me do exist, though most people can't even comprehend our role in society. The sheltered lives and insistent denial of the masses allow me to operate in plain sight. Despite 24-7 news coverage that depicts in living color how the world is literally burning, the average person remains oblivious about how such events come to pass. Most people naively assume that random chance or coincidence sets the wheels of global policy in motion.

I profit handsomely from this misconception.

Remember T.E. Lawrence? Yes, the legendary Lawrence of Arabia, the leader of the Arab revolt against the Turks during World War I, who was hired after the war by Winston Churchill to redraw the map of the Middle East and break up Mesopotamia into modern-day Iraq, Jordan, and Palestine at the Cairo Conference in 1921.

No, Mr. Lawrence, despite his ability to write history, was not a member of my profession. But one of his best friends, William Yale, a descendant of the founder of Yale University, was hired by Standard Oil of New York City to seek out new oil deposits in the Middle East prior to the war. Meeting T.E. Lawrence during his travels, the two quickly became close friends. Once the war began, the US Department of State hired Yale as their lone source of intelligence gathering in the region. Whatever Yale reported—and recommended—became US policy. Being so close to Lawrence made his influence at the time of the first

Great War immeasurable to the Americans. In international consulting circles, it's believed that Yale "suggested" to Lawrence where various boundaries should be drawn—and where certain oil might deposits lie. Later, as an expert on Middle East affairs, Yale became US President Woodrow Wilson's personal "adviser" for international relations in the region. But despite his contributions for altering US decision-making in the Middle East, he was never a government employee but rather just a paid international consultant with immense sway.

I share that bit of history as an example of how power and influence really work. It's not at the ballot box. Say what you will about conspiracy theories, but know this—they provide men like me with excellent cover from the truth. Take, for example, another famous incident involving an international consultant—"Operation Ajax" in Iran. Most history books will tell you that CIA Senior Operations Officer Kermit Roosevelt, Jr., grandson of US President Theodore Roosevelt, was responsible for overthrowing the Iranian Prime Minister Mohammed Mosaddegh in 1953. In fact, both the CIA and British intelligence service MI6 planned "Operation Ajax" after Mosaddegh nationalized the highly profitable Anglo-Iranian Oil Company (AIOC), which would later go on to become British Petroleum (BP). Most people fail to remember that the first attempt to overthrow Mosaddegh, and directing the Shah (King) of Iran Mohammed Reza Pahlavi to replace him with an appointed general who was friendly to US and British interests failed miserably.

Because of that botched attempt, the Shah was exiled to Italy for his own safety. The CIA and MI6 were left scrambling to pick up the pieces from their embarrassing mess. It was at this point that an international consultant was called in to salvage the pieces. I won't tell you the identity of the consultant, but his plan—although unorthodox—quickly and successfully rallied the citizens of Iran around their Shah and removed Mosaddegh.

Essentially, the consultant paid all the local street gangs and mafias to pose as supporters of Mosaddegh and conduct public acts of violence and disrespect to the Shah. This embarrassing, distasteful behavior was enough to outrage the Iranian population into believing that Mosaddegh and his nationalist party members were thugs. When the Shah returned from his brief exile to attempt once again to remove Mosaddegh, he easily succeeded. As a result, the Shah stayed in power for another twenty-six years until The Iranian Revolution in 1979. The CIA denied any involvement. Many years later, Kermit Roosevelt wrote a book about the coup, which was dismissed by his peers and never included the true story of the consultant who actually instigated the change in power.

If you're too young or poorly educated to recall those events, here's a more current example of one of my former competitors— yes, we international consultants do have our rivals to contend with.

Viktor Bout was, hands down, one of the most prolific arms dealers the world has ever known. He supplied Liberian President Charles Taylor with thousands of AK-47 assault rifles during the Sierra Leone Civil War. They even made a movie about it, *Lord of War*, starring Nicolas Cage. He was former Libyan dictator Muammar Gaddafi's go-to guy for heavy weapons procurement. He even played both sides of the war in Afghanistan by supplying the Northern Alliance and the Taliban with weapons at the same time. It was even rumored that he had Osama bin Laden on his speed dial. So successful at smuggling weapons from one conflict zone to another, he was nicknamed "Merchant of Death."

Despite his international fame, most government agencies still didn't know Bout's true place of birth or his background. He spoke six languages fluently and held numerous passports. Some believed he was born in Tajik, in the Soviet Union (now Tajikistan), while some intelligence services thought he was from the Ukraine. It was rumored he was previously in the KGB, yet others claimed it was the Soviet Air Force. One theory even described him as a childhood friend of Russian President Vladimir Putin.

I have my own ideas of Bout's true origins. We once spent four hours playing poker and drinking vodka in a penthouse suite in Dubai with a gaggle of Russian hookers. He bet the pot and lost—he still owes me that $70,000. Unfortunately, I will never see the money, nor will I learn Bout's true origins.

Viktor Bout broke the cardinal rule of being an international consultant—he got caught. The US Drug Enforcement Agency set him up in a joint sting operation. Thinking he was selling a submarine to guerillas from the Colombian Revolutionary Armed Forces (FARC), so that they could smuggle cocaine into the United States undetected, Bout was apprehended in Bangkok by the Royal Thai Police.

It was a bad day for Viktor, but a good day for me. While he rots away in a grimy Southeast Asian prison cell, it has allowed me to poach all of his clients and essentially double my annual sales. Of course, I fear the day when it could just as easily be me in that cell. But I like to think I'm different—though I'm sure everyone who has ever gotten caught has thought the exact same thing. The point, my friend, is this profession is very real. And it should come as no surprise that business is booming.

But don't be misled. Not all of us international consultants are hiding in the shadows, avoiding the likes of Scotland Yard and the FBI. In fact, you most likely know some of my more famous colleagues. For example, since he left office in 2007, former British Prime Minister Tony Blair has provided me tough competition in both Africa and Central Europe. In fact, Mr. Blair has amassed a consulting fortune of close to 100-million pounds by providing endorsements and other good public relations efforts for a handful of unpopular world leaders, including Muammar Gaddafi, as well as some other questionable clients in Nigeria and Kazakhstan.

But the greatest international consultant of them all—the gold standard if you will—is former US President William Jefferson Clinton. "Slick Willy," as he was known during his time in office, has set a new bar for international consultants. He has amassed well over $200 million in the past two decades, and he has done it all under a white-hot spotlight—and the world loves him for it. Fortunately for Clinton, not only does he have unfettered access to anyone on the planet, but he also has his "foundation," where he can safely park his profits. The guy is a true genius.

Like any consultant, I have my own methodology for doing business. The secret of my success is simple. It's also what separates me from my competition. It's that I understand the difference between information and intelligence. Though *information* is something that can be easily obtained, *intelligence* is critical knowledge that your enemies would prefer you not to know. I have always had a knack of acquiring this critical intelligence. I am always in the know. As such, I have become a very rich man, albeit a targeted one.

My life might appear mysterious and glamorous, but I must always move with caution. Just as I have built a satisfied list of clients, I have also accumulated an equal—or even greater—list of people who blame me for their downfalls and want revenge. They are probably right. Either way, I have climbed the greasy pole of international geopolitics to get where I am today.

\* \* \*

The pilot just announced that we will be touching down in thirty minutes. I will arrive at Washington Dulles International Airport as one person, but in two days I will depart the United States for Canada as someone else.

# KINGS
## I

# THE CLIENT

**Location:** *360 Restaurant, CN Tower, Toronto*
**Time:** *2057 hours*

Canada is a wonderful country. Even more wonderful is the freedom that a Canadian passport provides its owner. The document is the ultimate all-access pass for those wishing to travel the world without concern of visa restrictions or too many questions from local authorities. After a lovely dinner last night at the famous Café Milano in Washington's upscale Georgetown neighborhood, where I convinced an executive from the World Bank why he needed to provide my client—a struggling Central American country—with a $500 million loan, I jetted up to Toronto on my Canadian alias for a meeting at the 360 Restaurant atop the CN Tower.

You might think that in my business, meeting a prospective client at a public restaurant is a bad idea. Especially one located 116 stories above ground with only one way in and one way out. You might be right. But I'm a cautious man, so I have already considered the possibilities. I've been tracking the movements of my new prospect for the past forty-eight hours, both physically and electronically, and for several reasons I have chosen to meet him face-to-face at the revolving restaurant, which sits high atop the Toronto skyline.

First, anyone entering the tower must pass through extensive security—metal detectors complete with air puffers to detect explosive residue—designed to keep out anyone with weapons. Likewise, canine teams, undercover officers trained in body-language profiling methods, and a myriad of CCTV cameras ensure that if my client has brought a surreptitious backup team, those gentlemen will have to wait outside rather than risk being detected.

Second, hundreds of tourists move in and out of the tower daily, giving me cover in case I need to make a fast exit. I could even insert my own counter-surveillance professionals into the crowd. I wouldn't, because I always operate alone. But my prospect doesn't know that, so it gives him something to worry about.

I take comfort in that my lack of visibility creates worry among existing and potential clients. It gives me an edge—and in my line of work even the smallest advantage has value.

As Sun Tzu (actual name Sun Woo) said, "All warfare is based on deception."

Third, I entered the country on my handy Canadian passport. As a citizen of Canada—whether I am truly a citizen or not—I'll be able, if I have to, to quickly exit back across the border.

My prospect emailed me seventy-two hours ago to request a meeting. He found me via one of my previously satisfied customers, a wealthy and prominent Indian businessman whose son I had saved from going to prison. I helped bury an investigation after a Hungarian prostitute hired by the son mysteriously fell from the side of the father's yacht in the Bay of Bengal and drowned. But that's a story for another time.

His email was short and sweet:

*Tall Man,*

*I am in urgent need of your consulting services. You come highly recommended by The Indian. Can we meet as soon as possible? It will be worth your time.*

*M.*

My reply was equally simple:

*M,*

*Three days from now . . . 360 Restaurant, Toronto, at 2100 hrs. Come alone. Cash expected upfront. No tricks.*

*Abraham*

I'll let you in on a little secret. The email address I give out for others to reach me contains a clandestine sniffer program. With it, I can trace the source of incoming messages. True, most of those wishing to contact a man like me use a sterile or untraceable computer or IP address. But some don't, including this prospective client. You'd think the chief of staff for an African ruler would know better than to use his personal Gmail account to contact "Tall Man." But common sense is not always so common. His lapse in judgment allowed me to begin my due diligence before the meeting.

I quickly discovered that the chief of staff was also the half-brother of the king. I won't mention the name of the African country in question, because doing so could reveal some of the sources and methods of my work. In Africa, monarchies often teeter on the brink of revolution. And this so-called royal family was fighting for its survival.

After I hacked into the chief-of-staff's email, I learned he had booked his flight to Toronto via Paris. He had landed the previous night and was traveling with his twenty-two-year-old secretary, who was also his mistress. I filed away this information—along with the naked "selfies" they share with each other over Skype—for possible future use. More importantly, he had exchanged no communiqués with anyone suggesting logistical or security support while he was in Canada. So there was a good chance he was planning to meet me alone—something I demand for all first-time encounters.

My research further revealed that this fifty-three-year-old highly obese chief of staff, and his voluptuous young secretary, were staying at the opulent Fairmont Royal York. I surveilled them when they left the hotel and toured the nearby heart of town on foot. After several hours of shopping, strolling through the snow-lined parks, and lunching at a busy café, the couple returned to their room two hours before our dinner meeting.

The chief of staff departed the hotel at eight-thirty that night, alone in a taxi and headed for the restaurant. I knew that because I followed him in a chase vehicle, in this case a local taxi. He entered the CN Tower and proceeded through security.

I followed with my date, a savvy working girl I'd engaged from an upscale but very discreet escort service. We lingered roughly fifty meters behind him. I was using the girl as cover. If the chief of staff was using a counter-surveillance team to determine if he was being followed, or if I was being set up by Canadian law enforcement, most likely they'd be looking for a lone male that evening, instead of a well-dressed couple on their way to dinner. My female companion had no idea, of course, that I was tracking a quarry. As far as she was concerned, I was probably a married businessman looking for some excitement.

I led my date closer to the chief of staff as he walked into the restaurant. Then I turned to the young lady and slipped 200 Canadian dollars into her hand. I instructed her to wait by the elevators for ten minutes. If I didn't return to fetch her by then, she was free to depart. But if I did return, it meant I needed her services a bit longer. She probably thought I meant having dinner together followed by sex. But I'd be using her for a quick escape from the tower as a couple followed by crossing back into the United States alone by car.

As the chief of staff approached the maître d's stand, he spoke apprehensively. "Reservation for Abraham, party of two."

"Is your dinner companion here?" the maître d' asked.

"I am," I confidently said, sneaking up behind my would-be client.

"Ah, Mr. Abraham!" bellowed the round African man with a bright, toothy smile.

"That's me. But I regret I don't yet know your name." I lied; I had already established a detailed dossier on him and his family.

"I am Mohammed, and we have a great deal to discuss. I am so glad you decided to join me for this meeting on such short notice."

"I hope I can say the same by the time we're finished."

The maître d' showed us to a table along the edge of the grand window. The restaurant was slowly rotating to capture a magnificent, 360-degree vista of Toronto. The African grinned with delight. I wasn't sure if it was because he had managed to secure an audience with me or because he had never been this high up in a building before, especially one that moves.

"Shall we order champagne to celebrate this occasion?" he asked.

"I only drink champagne *after* I've completed a deal," I replied.

"This is just a preliminary meeting. Nothing yet to celebrate." I found myself becoming irritated with this obvious buffoon.

"We are going to celebrate my brother staying in power and you becoming a rich man. What else?" He could not stop smiling at me.

"Speaking of rich," I remind him, "I am charging a retainer just for this meeting."

"So you wrote in your email," his voice suddenly changing to a deeper, less pleasant tone. "But you did not state how much you charge."

I looked him straight in the eyes. "You obviously have a serious problem, or you would not have reached out to me. How much is it worth to you to have that problem resolved quickly and discreetly? That's how much I'm going to charge you. I don't charge by the hour, the day, or even the month—I charge by the crisis. How much did you bring? If it's the correct amount, I will stay and listen. If not, you're welcome to order champagne for yourself."

The chief of staff sat silent for a moment. Then he leaned toward me. "The Indian told me you were a serious man. . . and expensive." He reached into his suit pocket and retrieved a white envelope from the Fairmont Royal York. He slid it across the table.

*Damn, dumb amateur!* I thought to myself. *You don't slide cash envelopes across restaurant tables in full view of customers and staff—including possible law-enforcement or intelligence operatives!*

As if Providence was reinforcing my judgment, just then the waiter approached us. "Uh ... please let me know when you are ready to order your drinks, gentlemen."

I quickly collected the envelope and put it in my suit pocket.

"How much?" I asked curtly.

"So much that I promise you won't have to open it until you get to your bank. And there will be so much more to come that I insist we do order that bottle of champagne."

I gave him a nod, but inside I knew I didn't trust this guy any more than I could throw his fat ass.

"Tell me," he said. "I know your name is not really Abraham. Perhaps you think you are like Abraham Lincoln? Or maybe it is Abraham after the father of the three great religions—Islam, Christianity, and Judaism?"

His question was meant to disarm. But I knew I hadn't misjudged this character. He, like his brother, was in power for a reason. He might not be the most cultured person, but guys like this know what it takes to survive.

"It's just a name I use. . . no particular reason." In fact, I had a reason. But for now I'll keep it to myself.

Mohammed described the fragile situation in his country. Due to the proliferation of the internet and underground free-speech newspapers, along with movements for fair elections springing up in neighboring African countries, his brother's monarchy was suddenly in jeopardy. The idea of an African Spring, in which the masses would rise up to overthrow their corrupt and repressive governments, could be much more dangerous than the Arab Spring was to the rulers of the countries in the northern part of the continent.

Mohammed explained to me that the current situation could be quelled by silencing the leader of the opposition. A gentleman to whom he referred as "David" had been stoking the passion of the citizens by claiming it was time for democracy in the kingdom. David wanted to run against the king in an open election at the end of the year. His popularity was gaining momentum. He was an educated man with powerful friends in the West. He had given interviews to the global news networks and garnered the attention of Hollywood celebrities, some of whom began championing David's cause. The monarchy, rife with corruption scandals, human rights abuses, and severe wealth discrepancies between the royal family and average citizens earning less than two dollars a day, had fallen within the world's crosshairs.

This is exactly the kind of crisis calling for someone with my particular skills. In today's ever-changing geopolitical environment, many sitting government leaders and their political parties face threats to their stability. Declining public opinion, elite support from well-funded opponents, and the power of social media to sway mass opinion, all have led to the overnight demise of leaders, some of whom had held power for decades. Given such environments, it was inevitable that more Arab Spring-type uprisings would emerge throughout the Middle East, Africa, South America, and elsewhere.

Many political think tanks have concluded that issues of governance and legitimacy, coupled with organized protests via social media, will begin to reshape the world's political landscape in the coming years—although, as someone who operates "down in the mud" in most of these places, I have a different perspective than the academics. This is bad news for the corrupt leaders of the world, but it is good news for my competitors and me. Still, just as the door is shutting on some of the most ruthless dictators in the world, my time in their employ is also closing. This might be one of my last opportunities to cash in, and I planned on laughing all the way to the bank with Mohammed's money.

* * *

To solve the African's problem, I needed a plan. But I also needed look no further than the worn, torn, leather-bound book in my briefcase. *The Art of War*, the ancient treatise on strategy written around 500 B.C. by an unknown author, details the teachings of Chinese General Sun Tzu, and has been a constant companion of mine. I had received this particular copy several years earlier as a gift from a highly satisfied client in Singapore. I stole the data for a new technology that his largest competitor was about to release. My duplicated concept quickly beat his competitor to market—thus making billions in profits. You probably own the device yourself.

The point is, to an international consultant, *The Art of War* is our version of a playbook. It serves as a reminder of how human beings are predictable and can be manipulated. Its lessons are literally timeless, such as one of my favorite passages within those dog-eared pages:

*"If you know the enemy and know yourself, you need not fear the result of 100 battles. If you know yourself, but not your enemy, for every victory gained, you will suffer a defeat. If you know neither the enemy nor yourself, you will succumb in every battle."*

I never take on an assignment without knowing my opponent's next move before he does.

I looked across the table and noticed that Mohammed was eyeing me cautiously. I knew he was trying to figure out what I was thinking. I was certain that if we sat down together at a poker table, I would quickly discover his "tell"—that unconscious, reflexive behavioral sign everyone displays when he or she is lying. I just shot him a smile. One thing I have learned, and trained myself to practice to perfection, is never to let on what I am thinking, particularly to a client. I tried to put him at ease.

"Why don't we order that champagne now, Mohammed?"

"Does this mean that you will take the assignment, Mr. Abraham?"

I paused for a moment then leaned closer to him. "Two million dollars wired to an account of my choice within 24 hours and another two million after the job is done," I said softly.

Mohammed laughed. "Deal, Mr. Abraham, deal . . . but I'll have you know that I was prepared to pay double that."

"Don't worry, you will. Once I perform this first miracle, your government will want to keep me on retainer. And that will cost one million dollars, US, per year, just to have immediate access to my services. This does not include the individual project cost, nor my expenses. It only permits you to contact me at any time and guarantees I will respond within twenty-four hours."

"You are a very confident man, Mr. Abraham. I like that about you."

I stared at Mohammed stoically.

"*Très bien* . . . yes, let's order that champagne," he cheerfully bellowed, summoning the sommelier to our table.

"Good evening, sir," the man said in polished diction. "How may I assist you?"

"Please bring us a bottle of your finest champagne," Mohammed replied.

"Of course, sir. That would be our 1985 Dom Pérignon. It is fifteen-hundred dollars a bottle."

"Wonderful!" Mohammed said.

"Excellent choice, sir! I will be right back." The sommelier hustled away to fetch the bottle, and I could see a slight grin appear. He knew he had just earned a nice commission, plus tip, for doing next to nothing.

Meanwhile, Mohammed continued. "Tell me, Mr. Abraham,

how did you get into this line of work? You must have a military or intelligence background—or perhaps law enforcement at the most critical level. I want to know all about your history in the profession."

"I don't talk about myself," I replied.

Mohammed suddenly appeared irritated.

"That is not a good marketing strategy, Mr. Abraham. How do you expect to earn new business if you do not talk about yourself?"

"For the same reason we are enjoying this dinner together right now. When you are good, other people will do your bragging for you."

Mohammed threw his head back and laughed again, loudly, the way only a corrupt high official could. He apparently liked my answer. People at nearby tables began to stare.

The sommelier arrived with the fifteen-hundred-dollar-a-bottle champagne and displayed the label to his customer.

"Dom Pérignon, '85, sir," he said.

"Wonderful," Mohammed repeated, "and please have another one chilled for us to enjoy after our entrées."

I felt pleased, thinking of how many times I had been in this same situation over the years. Talking a client into a four-million-dollar deal over Dom Pérignon had become second nature.

# IN TRANSIT

*Location:* *Hyatt Regency London – The Churchill, Portman Square*
*Time:* *1400 hours*

I stood in the Hyatt Regency's lobby, staring eye-to-eye with a bust of Winston Churchill. I could almost imagine the old man saying to me, "What in bloody hell are you getting yourself into with these ruffians?" Then I noticed the doorman waving that my taxi was ready. I glanced back at Churchill and whispered under my breath, "You always said if you're going through hell— keep going."

I had flown to London from Toronto three days earlier, arriving at Heathrow on that same Canadian passport, after agreeing to take the job for Mohammed and his brother the king. I would need at least a week to collect intelligence and cover my tracks. After checking into my hotel, I showered and paid a visit to Savile Row and my eighty-two-year-old tailor, Nigel—or "Sir Nigel," as he is lovingly referred to by his loyal customers.

Having a suit made to measure is not only one of the finer pleasures in a man's life, but it also serves as the perfect cover for visiting a country briefly. A refined gentleman may fly into a city for only twenty-four hours to have a fitting. Immigration and Customs officials usually accept this justification for a quick layover. It provides a further excuse when the gentleman returns to pick up the garment—and possibly for a third time should alterations be needed.

After Sir Nigel measured me for a three-piece, navy-blue herringbone, super-150 wool suit, I headed to celebrity chef Jamie Oliver's Fifteen restaurant on Westland Place. I enjoyed a hearty lunch of mushroom ravioli and burrata cheese. I washed down my meal with only one glass of Chilean Carmenère wine, because I needed to keep my wits sharp. The British MI5 internal security service surveillance capabilities were becoming dangerous for me.

I returned to my room and spent the remainder of the evening conducting, via an encrypted router meant to disguise my IP address, open-source research about my new client and his kingdom. I quickly discovered that I would be dealing with a butcher. The king, like his father before him, was a heavy-handed leader who controlled through fear and intimidation. There were numerous occasions where his regime was accused of brutality by international human-rights organizations. Yet, somehow the king was always able to circumvent those allegations when a key witness suddenly went missing or, worse, turned up dead from an apparent "suicide."

The king's rival, Mr. David, appeared to be squeaky clean. He was an Oxford-educated human-rights advocate who previously served in a senior position with a UN-sponsored program in Africa. He left his home country to pursue higher education and promote agricultural initiatives and HIV/AIDS awareness across the continent. His address to the United Nations two years earlier made him the poster child for a more progressive Africa.

Meanwhile, the man in whose employ I agreed to enter has three wives, one of whom just turned seventeen. He is notorious for making absurd statements to the media—such as claiming to have eaten the hearts of his former enemies in order to make him stronger. And he is usually drunk or stoned twelve hours per day.

This assignment would not be easy—though I admit I like it that way.

The taxi ride from the hotel to the train station takes almost thirty minutes. It gives me time to reflect on my next move. I am taking the high-speed train—the TGV—and crossing the Chunnel on the Eurostar. I have swapped out my passports and will now travel as an Italian citizen into France. In addition to a new nationality, I will also be using a new name.

Upon arriving in Paris, I take a taxi to the famous Notre Dame Cathedral. With my rolling carry-on bag in tow, I might be any Western tourist being dropped in the heart of the City of Lights.

I snap a few touristy pictures to reinforce my cover and head across the Seine River towards the St. Germain section of town. I even shoot a few of those God-awful "selfies" that Brazilian tourists are always taking of themselves. Could there be a more undignified act? It's like masturbating in public. You might as well wear a sign that says: *I'm a loser!*

I walk up the block of each street in a stair-stepping fashion, which is to say that I am climbing up one and over one with each intersection. This allows me to look back and see if anyone is following. I stop at a crepe stand on the street for ten minutes and enjoy a banana and nutella crepe from a vendor. We chat about the weather in French, as well as the ugly American tourists roaming the monuments snapping pictures and asking stupid questions. I am soon back on my way. Exactly twenty-two minutes later I reach my destination.

The traditional seven-story French architecture building is adorned with gargoyle statues on the roof. Constructed in the time before elevators and air-conditioning, I climb five flights of stairs to a dark hallway. I knock on a nondescript door and am greeted by a striking, middle-aged woman with short, dark, silky hair. She is wearing only a black bra and matching panties. A lit cigarette is dangling from her full lips. *How French*, I think. She slaps my face hard without saying a word. *How very French.* She then immediately grabs my shirt and pulls me in for an even harder kiss. I love European women!

Lola is a flight attendant that I met several years ago en route to Hong Kong. She served me dirty martinis until I worked up the courage to ask her to dinner. Since then I have paid her several visits. However, my last visit was well over a year ago.

When she is not traveling the world catering to wealthy businessmen, Lola keeps an apartment in Paris. I will need to hide out for the night in her small studio, as I have chosen not to stay in a hotel for fear of being monitored by the French authorities. The French intelligence service—the vaunted DGSE—is extremely good at keeping tabs on foreigners in their hotels. Right now, I need to remain under the radar. I am sure that I'm not the first man to spend the night at Lola's apartment and I certainly won't be the last. Tonight she is providing me cover in more ways than one.

I wake up at five-fifteen the next morning. Lola is still fast asleep from all the wine and other activities we enjoyed last night. I take a shower and fix myself an espresso in her incredibly tiny kitchen. Why is everything so damn small in Europe? My carry-on bag is already packed and I sneak out the door without so much as a kiss on her forehead. Lola is still asleep and I leave her no note. We both prefer it this way. She will forget about me by lunchtime and I will forget about her the moment I step out onto the street from her building.

I walk two blocks from the apartment just to ensure some separation between Lola and myself. I don't need to be running into her should she suddenly arise and make her way out the door. I find a twenty-four-hour café and order a *croissant* and *café au lait*. I recognize that my French is a bit rusty—all that wine last night didn't help either—but no matter, because I'm going to fly to Africa today on my Italian passport anyway. My Italian is flawless. Feeling energized by the caffeine, I hail a cab and head to Charles de Gaulle Airport.

Flying out of CDG is a nightmare for travelers, but it is also a great way to hide in plain sight from prying intelligence services and law enforcement agencies. I once drew their attention when I traveled into Copenhagen using my Bahamian passport. Apparently, a fellow passenger thought that I was a narcotics trafficker and reported me to the authorities. Needless to say, I have never used that identity again. And for the record, I was moving diamonds—not narcotics. Being a drug mule is beneath a man of my skills.

I easily collect my first-class ticket from the Air France counter and make my way through the security check. I have no doubt that the inspectors can smell the red wine in my pores as they give me the cursory pat down, after my Patek Philippe watch sets off the magnetometer. These foolish men are so concerned about finding a weapon that they are oblivious to the fact that the gentleman, whose testicles they are currently cupping, can topple a nation with just a few phone calls and the swipe of a pen. I think to myself, *Sir, if you really wanted to slow me down you should be confiscating my rollerball Mont Blanc, not my eight-ounce Evian water bottle.*

I have passed security, and now it is time to stock up on a few tricks of the trade. I stop in the duty-free store and collect three bottles of Johnny Walker Blue off the shelf, three boxes of Cohiba Robusto cigars from the humidor, and three tubes of Toblerone chocolate (in case I need some help from children) from the candy aisle. I may need these as gifts in order to bypass some traditional African red tape. No one during my extensive travels has ever said no to the ultimate door opener—a wad of crisp Benjamin Franklins—which are always wrapped in a tight rubber band simply for effect.

Boarding the aircraft first, even before the elderly and parents with small children, I nestle into my usual preferred seat, 1A. I call this the power seat because everyone else has to walk past you while you drink champagne and most likely think, *Who is this dick?*

The flight to my client's country will take several hours. Therefore, I will take this opportunity to catch up on some much needed sleep. Unfortunately, since the plane's manufacturer is Airbus instead of Boeing, they do not have those little air jets above each individual chair. This means that the cabin, as is typical of all Air France flights, will be uncomfortably warm. Couple that with the fact that half the Frenchmen on the plane probably did not shower this morning. Perhaps I can take a sleeping pill with a glass of wine? No. That might leave me feeling too groggy to make a good first impression when I land. My best bet is to focus on the task at hand.

* * *

I start to rework my initial hypothesis of how I should handle this consulting situation in my head. Until I am able to ask more questions and get a feel for the situation on the ground, my game plan is still uncertain. I go back to my fundamentals of international consulting and prepare a list of clever buzzwords that I will use to impress the king and his immediate staff.

I will walk them through the steps of my consulting philosophy in order to educate them to the reality of the situation. My patented, yet unscientific, methodology consists of the following process:

*Identify the problem.*
*Clarify the scope of work.*
*Conduct due-diligence and intelligence gathering.*
*Perform assessments and analysis.*
*Form a hypothesis for a possible solution.*
*Integrate the proposed solution.*
*Test and verify the proposed solution.*
*Solve the problem.*
*Perform ongoing maintenance.*
*If all else fails, bribe, extort, or eliminate the problem.*

I smile as I think of how many times this simple process has made me a millionaire so many times over. It's really just common sense. Although I recognize that others may not think it's easy, it really is all about consistency and performing under pressure. Shooting a free throw in basketball is easy. But, not everyone can make two in a row when the championship is on the line and thousands of people are wildly screaming. Not every Harvard Law or Wharton MBA graduate can successfully negotiate the release of a hostage with radical terrorists wielding a gun to the victim's head, under a hard deadline. Not many international consultants can work in this particular business for twenty years and still be around to talk about it.

I crack open *The Art of War* to a random page and read the passage:

*To defeat your enemy, first offer him help so that he slackens his vigilance; to take, one must first give.*

Suddenly an idea pops into my head and I have to smile.

*Fuck it,* I tell myself.

I make eye contact with the long-legged flight attendant to get her attention.

"Could you please bring me an Old Fashioned on the rocks?" I coolly say to her.

It is time for me to meet the king and go to work. Mr. David is history!

# AFRICA

As the plane goes wheels down at this typical African airfield, the first thing I notice out the window is an old farmer standing in shin-high water on the wet grass just off the runway. He is leaning himself up on a homemade walking stick, as a shaggy goat stands attentively at his side. Apparently, the land around the asphalt landing strip is where he grows his crops—rice probably. It is an unimaginable sight for most people not accustomed to the third world. Shouldn't there be a security fence to keep the peasants and wild animals out of the way? Are there not international regulations about these things? The old man seems immune to the deafening roar of the massive engines less than thirty meters from where he stands. However, the jet wash is too severe and he is blown over like a lawn chair in a strong wind. He is quick to bounce back up as though this is not his first time it has happened to him. The goat stands unfazed chewing on grass.

There is no jet way, which extends out from the terminal and connects with the aircraft's main cabin door. Instead, I am to be the first passenger to disembark down a set of wobbly metal stairs that have been propped up against the plane's fuselage. The attractive flight attendant, who kept my cocktails refreshed during the flight, wishes me good luck and reminds me to call her the next time I'm in Paris. She is not sticking around this African hellhole on a layover. The plane is immediately departing. I could find more than one use for this girl, especially since I've used Lola's apartment too many times already. Right now, however, getting the flight attendant's phone number is going to prove much easier than traversing this hazardous set of stairs.

When I eventually step down onto concrete, a young gentleman in a black suit with a skinny black tie greets me. He looks like he could be the brother of Samuel L. Jackson's character in *Pulp Fiction*.

"Mr. Abraham, welcome, welcome. I am Amin," he tells me in a heavily-accented English.

"Hello, Amin," I reply.

"Mr. Mohammed would like to meet you right away. We shall drive to see him now. Yes?"

"Can we stop by the hotel first? I would like to freshen up before the meeting."

"Yes, yes. We will go to see Mohammed now."

I switch to French and explain that I would prefer to go to the hotel first. Yet once again he tells me, this time in French, that we will be going to see Mr. Mohammed *first*. That is the end of that discussion.

*Oh well,* I think. *It's not a big deal. I'm on the clock. Let's just get this consulting engagement started.*

I climb into the backseat of an armored black Land Rover SUV with my new friend Amin. As he starts the vehicle, a Beyoncé song blasts from the speakers. He quickly presses a button to cut off the music.

He smiles and says, "Sorry, I like Beyoncé very much; she has nice butt!"

"Yes, she does have nice butt," I agree.

That is the extent of our conversation during the drive.

Looking out the window, I see abject poverty. The roads are packed orange clay, electricity is scarce, and there are no stoplights. Malnourished humans stand around like zombies. Their clothes hang off them like skeletons. Cripples and beggars approach our car every time we come to a brief stop. Amin shoos them away with a flip of his hand. During my research of this place, official statistics put unemployment at 30 percent. However, as I am quickly discovering, that figure has to be closer to 80 percent.

As we turn a corner we begin to leave the starving crowds in our rearview mirror. The grass becomes greener and more manicured, and clean white paint begins to outline the buildings.

The SUV pulls into the driveway of a walled compound off the main road. The exterior resembles a fortress. The gates are pure steel painted a bright red. Amin honks his horn and the gate magically opens inward.

As we drive in, I see that the massive grounds resemble the finest manicured golf courses. There is a small pond with a fountain shooting a stream of water a few meters in the air. I see four athletically-built African girls in colorful bikinis playing a game of two-on-two volleyball at a court set up on the lawn. The road is lined with expensive pink brink pavers.

"Amin. Is this the king's palace?"

"No, this is Mr. Mohammed's residence."

The road ends at Mohammed's home. It is a two-story mansion that resembles the White House in Washington. Perhaps Mohammed has his own aspirations to be king one day. I file that potential lead away for another time.

Amin parks in front of the door of the impressive home. Immediately, Mohammed dances out with arms open to greet me. He is wearing a bright green, traditional robe, which is meant to keep him cool in the heat.

"Ah, Mr. Abraham, you finally made it! I am so happy to see you again my friend!"

"Thank you, Mohammed. I am so glad to see you as well."

Pleasantries are exchanged and Mohammed provides me with a short tour of his home. After seeing his well-stocked wine cellar, antique gun collection, in-home movie theater, and high-end fitness center, which obviously does not get a lot of use, I find myself on his back patio with cognac and cigar in hand, furnished to me by his elderly butler, who is sporting a crisp white servant's jacket.

The view is limited to his oval swimming pool, a few acres of fruit trees, and the four high walls of the compound. I am somewhat hoping that the volleyball girls are finishing up their game and decide to cool off with a swim. I feel very secure and comfortable—at least for the time being. Stevie Wonder's classic "Superstition" ironically plays from the outdoor speakers built into to the patio roof.

"Tell me, Mr. Abraham, do you have a plan to crush Mr. David?"

Mohammed is getting right down to business for once.

"I have a few ideas," I respond with confidence.

"I hope so. The king is getting very upset with Mr. David's continued disrespectful rhetoric in the media. Nobody insults my king! I am doing all I can to prevent Mr. David from having an unfortunate accident. If you do not solve this problem quickly and quietly, Abraham, I shall have to take matters into my own hands. This means that I won't be needing your services any longer and you may forfeit your payment."

"Mohammed, the job will get done when the time is right."

"What are you planning? Is it some kind of campaign to discredit his reputation? As you know Mr. David is a very moral person. There may not be a lot of—how do you say—"skeletons in his closet.""

"Trust me, Mohammed. I have been doing this for a long time. Everyone has something to hide."

"How about you? Do you have something to hide?"

"Of course, I do. That is how I have been able to stay in this business so long."Mohammed smiles widely and lifts his glass as if to make a toast.

"Tell me, Mr. Abraham. What is your secret to success? You obviously know things other men don't. I want to understand you and how you plan on keeping my king in power."

I can sense that Mohammed is trying to flatter me so that he can coax information from me. I decide to play along and just throw him some bullshit answer. This is a specialty of any good consultant.

"Well Mohammed, to win an election you essentially need to understand that an individual person is different from a group of people. The power of "groupthink"—the concept that we somehow comprehend less rationally as a collective member of society than we do as a lone person—is how politicians channel their message."

"I am afraid that I do not understand," he admits.

"It's simple. Everyone knows the difference between right and wrong. However, when we are included as part of a group, we somehow lose our way. It's like when you cut the line in a crowd because other people are doing it. You know it is wrong, but since others are also doing it, it allows your actions to somehow be justified. You don't have the guilt."

"And this will help my brother win how, exactly?"

I have underestimated Mohammed. Perhaps he has more common sense than I initially believed.

I continue my lecture. "At the end of the day, citizens vote for a candidate for essentially three reasons, and three reasons only:

"They recognize the candidate's name on the ballot—probably from a political ad or from overhearing a conversation about them—and/or have been told who to vote for ahead of time by unions, family members, the media, colleagues, teachers, etc.

"They believe the candidate will improve their personal situation.

"They simply like the candidate more—they pass the 'which candidate would you rather sit down over a beer with' test.

"In fact, for all the time, money, and effort that go into a presidential election, victory—in most cases—still comes down to which candidate ran a more effective campaign."

"Ah, I am beginning to understand now," says Mohammed, "You plan on running a more effective campaign for my brother?"

"Ha!" I laugh, which surprises Mohammed. "On the contrary, Mr. David is already running a campaign that is far superior to anything that me, your brother, or David Axelrod (President Obama's campaign manager) could put together."

"Then what exactly is your plan?" asks a confused Mohammed.

"Submission," I whisper back to him for effect.

Mohammed sits in stunned silence for a moment attempting to process what I just said. He then breaks into a hearty belly laugh, throwing his head back in his chair. He obviously likes my answer.

"Tomorrow, I shall take you to meet the king. And then you, Mr. Abraham, will rid us of our political opponent forever!"

I neglect to warn him to be careful what he wishes for. I hear a loud splash and then giggling. The girls have decided to jump in the pool after all.

# HIS MAJESTY

*Location: The Royal Palace*
*Time: 1003 hours*

After my discussion and drinks with Mohammed yesterday—followed by lively conversations with the volleyball girls—Amin drove me to my hotel. I am staying at the country's finest luxury establishment, which would be considered two-star accommodations in any first-world nation. Because the reservations were made under Mohammed's name, I of course, am given the penthouse suite, which in this case simply means that I have a room with both a living room and bedroom, high atop a rundown four-story building. The moldy wallpaper that adorns the room is bright red, while the water that flows out of the faucets is a soupy brown color. This is still Africa.

I slept fairly well last night. Although I always try to start my day with a swim, typically one-mile in the pool of whatever five-star hotel I'm staying in, I have little faith that the outdoor pool of this shoddy establishment is free of fungi, bacteria, and God knows what other yet to be discovered disease is in there. I opt instead to knock out 100 push-ups, 100 sit-ups, 100 air-squats, and 100 "burpees" (up and downs) in the ample-sized living room. Because I travel so much, and enjoy my food and drink, it is important that I try to get in a good calorie-burning sweat each morning. My breakfast of salmon eggs Benedict, French bread with orange marmalade, yogurt, fresh squeezed carrot juice, and Lavazza espresso was surprising edible. I ask the waiter who is cooking in the kitchen only to discover that the chef was recruited from the prestigious L' Hermitage Hotel in Monte Carlo (he must be paid a fortune to be working here in this country). I'm dressed in my finest 5,000 euro custom-tailored Brioni suit, and my 1,000 euro Ferragamo shoes are polished to perfection. It's not every day I get an audience with a king; it's more like twice a year for me these days.

I push through the revolving door of the hotel lobby into the humid, tropical climate of this shithole country. It's still early in the morning, but I know that within just a few hours' time, my suit will become sweaty and uncomfortable. That's when the mosquitoes start to swarm and the chance for malaria increases. Good thing I am taking my doxycycline pills as a prophylaxis.

I notice that Amin is parked with the Land Rover directly in the circular driveway. He must be assigned to me for the duration of my trip. This is both good and bad. Good in a sense that I will always conveniently have a ride available and bad because he can always keep tabs on my comings and goings.

After a short drive through the city, I now find myself at the royal palace, seated right outside his majesty's office. As I look around the opulent waiting area, I see numerous pictures of the king's father—the previous king—hanging on the walls. In one picture he is wearing his crown and royal jewels. In yet another, he wears traditional native garb in order to look like a man of the people. In another, he dons a safari suit waving to the crowd from a convertible Cadillac. About the only thing that each picture has in common is that the king is wearing his 1980s mirrored aviator sunglasses. In my experience in Africa (which includes pretty much every country), I have found that the only real prerequisite for being king is that you have to look good in your sunglasses . . . and even that rule can be overlooked if you're ruthless enough.

Sitting across from me is whom I can only assume is the king's bodyguard. This guy is as big as a wardrobe chest. He is roughly thirty years old and easily 300 pounds of solid muscle. In fact, I can see his muscles bulging from underneath his silver suit, which is far too small for him. His neck is nonexistent and he has rolls of meat on the back of his bald head. I imagine that he must have been plucked from some African village after he won a tribal hand-to-hand combat competition. But he is no primitive tribesman. A 9-mm Beretta handgun hangs from a shoulder holster underneath his tight jacket. He's probably received advanced weapons training from either the Brits or South Africans, which is par for the course in this part of the world. If he is lucky, he might have even by trained by a former Rhodesian soldier. I have found the "Rhodies" to be especially tough. The funny thing is, this man-child has his face intensely buried in his cell phone playing the phone app, Angry Birds. If an army were to storm the palace right now, there's a good chance that this guy might miss it.

A buzzer goes off and a red light above the king's door begins to flash. To the big man across from me, it seems like nothing out of the ordinary is happening. A strikingly beautiful and athletic African girl, who introduces herself as "Destiny," walks out of the king's office and informs me that his highness will see me now. I might not be wrong in assuming that she was either her nation's representative for the Miss Universe contest or a stripper plucked out of one of the local Lebanese-owned gentlemen's clubs. Those girls usually go onto administrative jobs for high-ranking government officials after their pageant/dancing days.

I gladly follow the girl's shapely figure into the office, which is more of a ballroom than workspace. At the far end of the room, I see the king sitting at a colossal wooden desk. It is so big that a small family could actually live inside it. Across from the desk are two ordinary leather chairs. Mohammed is sitting in one of them.

"Ah, Mr. Abraham. Thank you for coming," says a cheery Mohammed. "Allow me to introduce to you His Majesty."

Following international protocol where a person of higher stature receives the person of lesser authority, and using a regal voice, Mohammed turns to the king and announces, "Your Highness, please allow me to introduce you to our new consultant, Mr. Abraham."

I bow my head.

"Your Majesty," I begin, "it is my sincerest honor to meet you. Thank you for this opportunity."

The king remains seated in his chair and returns the nod without saying a word.

Mohammed jumps in immediately, "Your Highness, as I told you before, Mr. Abraham comes highly recommended. In fact, it may be fair to say that he is the finest consultant available in his chosen profession."

Once again, the king simply nods.

"Your Majesty, if I may?" as I point to the seat.

The king points to the chair, instructing me to sit.

"Sir, I believe that I have an idea that may be of value to you. However, it may initially sound a bit unconventional compared to what you're used to."

The king turns to Mohammed and declares, "Leave us."

"What?" says a confused Mohammed.

"I want to talk with this man alone."

Mohammed looks dejectedly at the king, looks at me, and then quietly excuses himself from the room.

The king looks back at me and demands, "Tell me about this plan of yours."

For the next twenty minutes I describe to the king how I am going to bring down his opponent. The king asks no questions. He merely nods occasionally, while never breaking eye contact with me. For an older gentlemen whose health is fading, he has the presence of a regal lion. Although I do this for a living, I catch a few drops of sweat nervously forming on my forehead. It has been a while since I've been intimidated during a presentation. I hope the king is buying what I'm trying to sell right now. I trust that my discussion with the king is going well, although he offers no words of encouragement. After it is clear that I have laid out my strategy and am open to questions, the king simply says to me, "That will be all."

Not certain if I have been hired or fired, I get up from my chair to depart the room, but not before bowing to his majesty. As my hand is on the doorknob to his office, the king offers me one more breath of instruction.

"Mr. Abraham, you will crush David for me."

"Yes, Your Majesty."

I have the feeling I cannot let this man down; otherwise, I will be the one who ends up getting crushed.

\* \* \*

Later that evening, my Beyoncé-loving driver Amin drops me off at the finest restaurant in town. He tells me that he will be back in two hours to collect me. This small French-Vietnamese establishment has been around for nearly forty years. The owners emigrated to what was then a sleepy little outpost, carrying their life savings on their backs.

I enjoy cod brochettes with spicy pepper sauce and puffed rice cakes for an appetizer. My entrée consists of sea bass and fried rice. I chase it all down with a bottle of fine pinot grigio. Dessert is a glass of port and a Partagas Cuban cigar. Brazilian bossa nova music is playing in the background. I laugh and think *that the real "Girl from Ipanema" has probably never been to this country.* It has been a long day and I am ready to retire for the evening.

I head back outside to the car, only to find Amin napping in the driver's seat. Beyoncé's mellow ballad, "If I Were a Boy," is softly playing from the speakers. The sight of the imposing tree trunk of a man, dozing off to a chick tune, makes me shake my head in bewilderment. I am convinced that this is one of those rare moments that I won't soon forget. *Only in Africa.*

I insert the brass key into my hotel room door and immediately know that something is amiss. The lights are on and I can hear the television blaring in the bedroom. I think to myself that it must have been done by housekeeping during evening turndown service. Walking deeper into the room, I hear a voice from the bedroom.

"Finally, you're home."

"Who's there?" I ask.

I peek inside the bedroom to see the king's secretary sitting up in my plush bed watching a movie. She is still in the same dress she was wearing early in the day, but her shoes are kicked off and she is obviously making herself comfortable.

"I'm sorry," she says. "His majesty informed me that you did not bring a secretary with you and that you may be in need of my services."

I stand in the doorframe of the bedroom with a perplexed look on my face. I wasn't sure of what to make of the king's offer.

He was either being completely serious or completely ironic. The girl was obviously sent to be a welcoming gift for me, but more importantly, as insurance for the king by putting me in a compromising position at a later date.

"Destiny," I respond, "I am flattered by the king's generous offer. However, I don't think that I will be requiring your services during my visit here. Please tell His Majesty that he is too kind. Perhaps I will call you if I need a memo typed up."

The girl looks disappointed, but she's also smart enough to know what is happening here. Just for good measure, I say the following line for the hidden cameras installed in at least three places in my room.

"The king is a good man whom I have great respect for. I am sure that he would never do anything that wasn't for the greater good of his people and his nation. May he serve the kingdom for many years to come."

I turn sideways in the doorway to demonstrate that it is time for her to leave. Like a well-trained actress, she picks up her shoes and exits the stage on cue. Her performance is over and I am even more cautious of his majesty than ever. It reminds again why guys like this hold power. I know plenty of businessmen, politicians, and military officers who have been blackmailed for their sexual improprieties. As attractive as Destiny is, there would be a good chance that pictures—or videos—of us together could later be used against me. I have no doubt that the king has a database of people that he has compromised.

After a hot shower I climb into the king-size bed and kick the numerous throw pillows onto the floor from underneath the comforter. I turn off the light on the nightstand and lay on my back staring at the ceiling in the dark. If I don't come through for the king, there is a good chance that I won't leave this shitty country alive. I close my eyes and smell Destiny's perfume on my pillow. Maybe I shouldn't have passed up her offer. If I don't succeed in my assignment, that might have been my last opportunity to enjoy intimacy with a woman.

# MEMBERS ONLY

**Location:** *The Royal Tennis Club*
**Time:** *0735 hours*

I wake up early the next day with a plan to finally meet Mr. David. I had to see what this man was all about. It's well known that he enjoys a game of tennis each morning at the members only Royal Tennis Club located in the upscale diplomatic quarter. Of course, the club is gated behind a three-meter-high wall adorned with razor wire. Amin dutifully drives me through the gate in the Land Rover and along a palm tree lined gravel driveway. The grounds are freshly manicured and the smell of cut grass is in the air. It reminds me of the pitch you might find at a famous football club, such as AC Milan or Manchester United. The car drops me off in front of a bright white colonial-style clubhouse. I feel like I have been transported back in time fifty years.

A valet dressed in a gold jacket and very Moroccan-looking fez cap opens my door for me. He greets me with, "Good Morning, Mr. Abraham. Welcome to the RTC." The manager of the club has obviously been notified of my visit today. This could be a problem and I hope that he has not informed any of his staff about me.

After a double espresso in the bar, I make my way to the locker room in order to change into my athletic wear. Tipping the towel boy for information, I learn that Mr. David has a match scheduled with the Ambassador from Côte de Ivory on the exclusive clay court, which is isolated far from the other courts in a discrete section of the grounds. Apparently, many high-level meetings take place here. Since the country is absent of any golf courses, it suddenly makes sense that this is the place where sportsmen come to conduct business. I decide to wander over.

With my racquet in hand as if to say, "I have winner of the next match," I sit on a spectators' bench across the court and watch as Mr. David and the Ambassador begin their game. Mr. David is highly competitive. Although he is twenty years younger in age to the senior diplomat, he shows no respect or mercy. He is determined to win every point possible. To Mr. David, this is not just a random game or simple form of exercise between two friends. He is attempting to dominate. He purposefully makes the less mobile ambassador unnecessarily chase the ball from side-to-side. It is almost like watching a cat play with a mouse before he kills it. I have seen men like this before. His weakness is his arrogance and ambition, which really translates into a hidden insecurity. The thought of this discovery makes me smile.

After thirty minutes, the ambassador mercifully begs for no more and the match is finished. He is sweating and wheezing profusely, as if five more minutes of this onslaught might trigger a heart attack. The ambassador walks toward the net to shake Mr. David's hand. Mr. David is not interested in sportsmanship and instead makes his way towards the court's exit off to the side. This guy is an even bigger prick than I thought. He is just the kind of opposition I enjoy bringing down.

As David exits the court, I approach.

"Mr. David?"

He looks me up and down cautiously.

"My name is Michael Douglas," I lie.

I've always liked the name Michael Douglas for two reasons. One, it is so generic that it returns literally thousands of search hits when you perform an internet query; and, two, I enjoy the actor Michael Douglas and his portrayal of Gordon Gekko in the movie *Wall Street*. I often draw inspiration from the fictitious Gekko character when I'm performing my international negotiations.

"I'm a correspondent for the *International Herald Tribune*. "What a nice coincidence to run into you like this," I continue.

"Hello," he responds, even more cautiously.

"If I had known you were a member of this club, I would have asked to meet you. My paper and I are big proponents of what you are trying to achieve in this country. In fact, I am doing a story entitled 'Is an African Spring Coming?' I would love to interview you."

A wave of confidence comes over Mr. David and his demeanor changes from one of caution to opportunity.

"Of course. I would be happy to speak with you. How about over breakfast inside the club?"

Trapping Mr. David is easier than spearfishing in a barrel.

"That would be wonderful," I reply.

Thirty minutes later we are seated at a table on the second floor of the club, which overlooks the many tennis courts below. Mr. David and I have both showered and dressed for the day ahead. He is wearing an Italian custom-tailored suit and sporting a gold Rolex, while I am dressed as an international reporter, which means jeans with a button-down oxford shirt, a navy blazer, and alligator loafers with no socks. Even though I don't require glasses, I am wearing rimmed tortoise frames. I easily look the part of the liberal newspaper do-gooder ready to concoct a propaganda piece on this future political hero. I even have my MacBook open and ready to take notes.

Mr. David begins like an old pro who is very familiar with dealing with the press.

"Mr. Douglas, before we begin, would you please mind showing me your media credentials? One can never be too careful as to who he gives an interview to."

"Of course, Mr. David. I respect your thoroughness. In fact, most world leaders that I interview make it a point to do the same."

I reach into my wallet and pull out a counterfeit ID card for the *International Herald Tribune*, which Mr. David pretends to inspect as if he knows what an IHT ID card looks like. He hands it back satisfied.

"Very well, Mr. Douglas. What would you like to know?"

"Well," I begin. "Would you please tell our readers why you

think the time is right for the monarchy in this country to be disbanded?"

Mr. David begins to pontificate on his political position. I pretend as if I am enthralled by every word he says. In some way I am, because it is a window into unlocking this man's personality and true intentions. However, I fully recognize that with each sentence he spits out, he is only repeating the same rehearsed talking points that he has bloviated several hundred times before. Nonetheless, I am supposed to be an objective journalist who is going to win international recognition for bringing these revolutionary ideas to the masses. I continue to play along until he finally looks at his expensive watch and decides the interview is over.

"Thank you, Mr. David," I say with false sincerity.

"No, no . . . thank you, sir. And I do hope that you don't misquote me or twist my words for your own personal gain," he says, with the sternness of a man who has been burned before by the press.

I see this as an opening for my true intentions.

"Mr. David, you have my word as a professional. I would never do that to you. In fact, why don't I do this: Why don't I let you see the article before it goes to print? Does that sound fair?"

This is an untraditional consideration provided by a journalist for sure. It certainly has never been offered to Mr. David before. However, how could he refuse? I inform him that if he would provide me with his email address I will email him the article for his approval prior to its submission to my editor. Mr. David provides me with his email address and I agree to send it over within twenty-four hours. The trap has been set, now I just need him to step his foot inside of it.

I spend the rest of the afternoon at the RTC. It is by far one of the nicest establishments in the country. There is no need to venture outside and experience the reality of extreme poverty that exists just outside the club's fortress-like walls. I find a comfortable couch with a coffee table in the corner of the lounge and begin to compose my fake news story about Mr. David. It isn't exactly my best work, but then again it will never be published anyway. Ninety minutes later, the article is complete. Time for a drink.

I attempt to get the bartender's attention, but he is too fixated on a televised women's tennis match between Maria Sharapova and Serena Williams. These professional women are something of an enigma. Women in this conservative country would never play tennis; much less show off that much skin. I briefly think that I may be supporting the wrong side. Maybe I should allow Mr. David to open this country up to more modern viewpoints and freedoms. Then I think about how much the king is paying me and I quickly shake that thought from my mind. I instruct the bartender to fix me a Manhattan on the rocks.

My one drink in the bar ends up being four. After a generous tip, I ask the bartender to call me a cab back to my hotel. I still have more work to do tonight.

I am back in my hotel room and have my computer booted up once more. Using a special USB drive, I save my new document to it. I then send Mr. David an email to the address he provided:

*Mr. David,*

*It was an absolute pleasure to meet you this morning. Thank you for your time. You are truly a man of great vision. As promised, I have just completed the article and attached it for your review. Perhaps we can meet for breakfast again to discuss?*

*Best regards,*

*Michael*

I do not attach the real document but rather a blank one. I then head down to the hotel restaurant to enjoy dinner and a bottle of wine.

When I return to my room, there is a response from Mr. David waiting for me.

Michael

It was a pleasure meeting you as well. However, the attachment you sent was blank. Could you please resend?

Thank you

David

Laughing, I reply:

Hmmm. . . ? My apologies. Not sure why you can't open it. Perhaps I can just pass it to you tomorrow morning at the club?

Thanks!

Mr. David responds with a simple:

Sounds good.

My operation is moving forward as planned.

* * *

The next morning, I arrive at the club extra early to seek out my towel boy from the previous day. I don't want Mr. David to see me. He may have done his homework and discovered that I don't actually work for the *International Herald Tribune*. He may have also asked the manager about me and was told that my name is Abraham and not Douglas. Therefore, it would be dangerous if I had to confront him again.

Once I find the towel boy, I instruct him to simply walk up to Mr. David and tell him that I had to leave early this morning. He will also hand Mr. David an envelope. Inside the envelope is the USB thumb drive with the news article. I give the towel boy twenty American dollars and tell him that he will get another twenty the next morning from me, provided he does his job today. If the boy does his job correctly, and Mr. David takes the bait, I will never return to this club again.

I wait in the parking lot in the SUV with Amin. A short time later, I watch as Mr. David's car pulls through the front gate. The fate of this nation, and its king, now hangs in the balance of a towel boy.

# OVERBOARD

*Location:* *The Royal Marina*
*Time:* *0907 hours*

With Mr. David at the club playing his morning tennis match against yet another lesser opponent, Amin drops me at the Royal Marina to have breakfast with Mohammed. The fact that the king dismissed Mohammed from our meeting the other day obviously has him worried. As chief of staff, it may be that his ego is bruised, but also he wants in on the plan for Mr. David. He unfortunately is going to be disappointed. In Africa, you are either in the loop or out of the loop. And it can be perilous for those who are excluded from knowing secrets.

Since this is a social get together, I came bearing gifts—a bottle of Johnny Walker Blue Label and a box of the Cuban cigars. Although it is probably pretty easy for Mohammed to obtain these items himself, it demonstrates that I come in peace and acknowledges his refined tastes.

I walk along the pier of the small marina in my tan Brioni linen suit with just a T-shirt underneath. I am not wearing socks with my alligator skin loafers. I feel like a Don Johnson wannabe from the old *Miami Vice* television show.

There cannot be more than three-dozen boats stored here—mostly fishing boats belonging to the various embassies for recreational use. However, at the end of the dock is, without a doubt, the mega-yacht belonging to the king. I won't reveal to you the name of 150-plus foot vessel, but I will tell you it refers to a famous Arabic poem. Tied up directly beside the king's mega-yacht is Mohammed's boat. It is far smaller in comparison— probably seventy-five feet—but still very respectful and very expensive. I estimate that it costs at least USD 3 million. Unlike the king, who christened his ship with an honorable title from traditional Muslim lore, Mohammed's yacht is named *Tits*.

"Permission to come aboard?" I call out.

Mohammed appears from behind a sliding glass door at the stern of the boat. He is wearing a tight white polo shirt, which accentuates his large belly, and white Bermuda shorts. The bright white clashes against his dark skin. He has cheap plastic flip-flops.

"Ah, Mr. Abraham!" He bellows in his deep African voice. "Welcome, welcome! I am so happy that you could join me for breakfast."

I walk over a floating plank and onto the impressive yacht.

"I brought you these, but it may be too early to enjoy them," I say, as I hand him the Scotch and cigars.

"Nonsense! The finer things in life should be enjoyed anytime."

Just as Mohammed speaks, three beautiful African girls appear in bikinis from inside the cabin. Each one is prettier than the next. They are not the same volleyball girls from the other day. I notice that one of them is the girl from the Skype selfies I pulled off Mohammed's computer. Mohammed must have teams of women on his payroll.

"I believe in three things: fine food, fine wine, and fine women, but not necessarily in that order," Mohammed says.

He laughs at his own joke. The girls, who didn't seem to understand what he just said, also giggle along like they have been trained.

Mohammed invites me to sit around a teakwood table for breakfast. He takes a chair across from me and the girls fill in the remaining seats. I now have one lovely young lady on each side of me and I can smell their cocoa-butter sunscreen lotion. The place settings are over the top. The utensils are gold-plated and the china has the name of the yacht engraved in gold script. The gaudy extravagance of African leaders never ceases to amaze me.

"Let's have some coffee," Mohammed says casually.

He claps his chubby hands together and a waiter in a white outfit appears with a golden coffeepot to fill our cups. Just as the hot coffee is pouring out, I hear a roar of the massive engines. The boat is starting up. Surely we cannot be going out to sea?

"Mohammed," I say nervously, "We are not going out on the water now, are we?"

"But of course, Mr. Abraham. What good is a boat if it only sits in the harbor?"

This is upsetting news. In my experience, being in the middle of the ocean with a corrupt and devious African leader is never a good scenario. Bad things always happen!

I quickly think up a lie.

"I am so sorry to tell you this, but I get painfully seasick on boats. It is taking all my strength right now just to sit here tied up at the dock. I am afraid that I must leave you. My apologies."

"I'm sorry, too, Mr. Abraham. But we have a meeting scheduled this morning and we are going to have it out on the water for security reasons. You of all people should surely understand this concept. Now just relax. I'm sure the ladies here can help take your mind off your maritime issues."

The girls give me a collective look that translates to, "You're pathetic." I could not care less about them.

Before I can object any further, the first mate—a boy no older than fifteen—unties the heavy ropes for the dock's pylons. We are moving. I think about trying to jump back on the dock, but it would be too dangerous of a leap. Besides, there's no telling what Mohammed might do out of surprise or retaliation. I decide to play it cool.

"I will do my best to hold down my food, Mohammed. Please just assure me that we will come back soon. As you know, I am working hard for His Majesty."

"That is precisely what we need to talk about, Mr. Abraham."

The food is served: cheese crepes, fruit, and chocolate croissants. The good news is that I have lost my appetite out of fear, which reinforces my cover story that I'm supposed to be getting seasick. I pick at it just to be polite.

Once we clear the breakwater at the marina, the boat begins to accelerate. We are heading out to sea at around thirty knots, an impressive speed for a craft this large. Fortunately, the ocean is calm. In the back of my mind, I begin to contemplate the need to jump overboard and swim back to shore. I try to stay cool in front of Mohammed.

"Now, Mr. Abraham. I understand that you had breakfast with Mr. David yesterday. I will need to know what you talked about." Mohammed says in a very direct tone.

I decide to be straight up with him. "You are correct. We did have breakfast yesterday. I was trying to elicit information from him so I could possibly use it against him."

"And did you succeed in your objective?"

"I believe I did," I respond confidently.

"Good, because I would hate to think that we are paying you all of this money for nothing." He lets out a bellowing laugh.

"I'm worth every penny," I calmly reply.

His mood suddenly turns dark, almost evil.

"Mr. Abraham. Please know that both of our reputations are on the line here. If you succeed, then I look good. If you don't succeed . . . well, let's just say you had better succeed."

He turns abruptly in his chair and claps his hands again. From out of the cabin comes the waiter again. However, this time that waiter is aggressively leading a man—who looks like a prisoner with his arms tied behind his back—through the sliding doorway. Although his face is bruised and beaten and he has silver duct tape across his mouth, I recognize him. It is the manager from the tennis club who greeted me upon my arrival the other day.

"You see Mr. Abraham, this man here did not succeed," Mohammed explains.

The restrained man is sweating and nervous. There is fresh blood around his nose, as well as a fresh urine stain on his pants. It is all too apparent that he understands his pending fate.

Mohammed continues his lecture.

"I told this man that you would be visiting the Royal Tennis Club as my guest. He was instructed to keep your visit very quiet. It has come to my attention that he has shared the news of your visit into this country with the local French Intelligence officers working out of the French Embassy. He is. . . what is the word? He is an 'asset' for the DGSE."

"What?" I utter.

*Just great!* I think to myself. *Now the French Intel service probably has me under surveillance and they are probably in my hotel room right now going through my things.*

"This man was recruited by the French to report on the VIPs who are members of the tennis club. It makes sense, of course. They pay him a few hundred dollars per month and he provides them with information about the discussions that take place between our country's elite. Such is how intelligence gets passed. However, this fool thought that our own internal security service would not find out about it. Little does he know that I oversee all internal security here in the kingdom. He was also working as my own asset and he didn't even know it. Now, he must pay for his crime of treason."

With just a nod of his head, the young first mate appears at the back of the boat with a large plastic bucket. With a scoop of some sort, he begins scooping out a thick red substance and tossing it into the water. He is throwing chum—basically chopped up fish—and blood into the water. The only time you would do this is when you are fishing for sharks. The hostage also sees this and releases a muffled scream from underneath his duct-taped mouth.

"Mohammed," I object, "far be it from me to tell you how to run your country, but you cannot do this! If this man has broken the law, then he must be tried in a court. Either way, I don't want any part of it. That's not what I'm being paid for."

"Be quiet, Mr. Abraham! Your weakness severely disappoints me. I thought you knew how Africa worked. Perhaps I need to throw you over the side of the boat as well."

"I understand how things get done in Africa better than anyone," I strongly respond. "But this is only going to draw unnecessary negative attention to you and His Majesty. You don't need another investigation, another scandal, prior to the election. Killing this man only serves as another distraction from all of the positive things that the king has accomplished. By putting this man in prison instead, you can make the claim in the media that he is working for the French Intelligence Service to bring down the monarchy on behalf of Mr. David. Hell, I can spin this so that it appears Mr. David is selling out his own people in order to turn the country over to the French for colonization. I can paint a picture that says the citizens will be slaves and Mr. David will be nothing but a puppet of the French! I can use this man as what we call a patsy—a tool for our political bidding. Keeping him alive is actually good for us right now."

Mohammed takes a moment to comprehend everything I just said. This could definitely be used as leverage against Mr. David. For someone like me, it is an opportunity to paint the king's political opponent as working for the French spy agency. It would make a delicious story that could be picked up by the worldwide cable networks. I begin to formulate a media strategy in my head that would make Karl Rove—President George W. Bush's chief political architect—smile with envy.

"Perhaps you are right, Mr. Abraham. After all, you are our expert consultant. This is why you get paid the big bucks." He begins to laugh again at his own joke.

The manager of the tennis club is beginning to sob. Sharks have been attracted by the scent of the blood in the water. At least three dorsal fins are circling behind the boat.

Mohammed points at the waiter to move the captive towards the stern. The captive resists. He is punched in the stomach by the waiter and doubles over.

Dragged to the back of the boat and now on his knees, the desperate man tries to plead for mercy through his gagged mouth.

Mohammed picks up the bucket of chum and dumps the remaining blood and guts over the condemned man's head.

"Stand him up." Mohammed instructs the waiter, whose white serving outfit is now smeared with fish blood.

"Today is your lucky day, my friend. If it were not for Mr. Abraham here, I would certainly throw you over the boat right now and watch these sharks feed on you while you scream. However, I am going to see you become a patsy in an international spy scandal instead, which will bring great shame to Mr. David. Although I promise you, when it's over, you will have preferred that I simply threw you to the sharks."

The man breathes a sigh of relief from under his duct tape. I, too, catch my breath for the first time in minutes.

"Mr. Abraham, you just saved this man's life."

"No sir, you did," I reply.

Mohammed looks at me, looks at the girls, who seem unfazed, and looks back at the relieved victim.

"I trusted you like a brother," he says under his breath to the still frightened man.

Suddenly, Mohammed raises his thick leg and kicks the man over the back of the boat. Everyone else is shocked stiff. One of the girls screams.

The man tumbles backwards into the sea. A few seconds later he bobs to the surface, fighting to get some air into his nostrils. The sharks begin to circle. Shrieks of intense fear are heard for just a few seconds. Then he vanishes for good under the reddish water.

"What the fuck was that?" I yell.

"I changed my mind." Mohammed says casually. "Besides, I know that you already have a plan to destroy Mr. David. Why don't we just stick with that idea?"

With that, Mohammed walks back to the breakfast table and collects the three girls to go inside with him.

He turns to me and asks with a smile, "How is your stomach doing?"

The four of them vanish into the cabin.

The young boy starts mopping up the fish blood. The waiter begins to clear the dishes from the table. I am left standing on the back of the boat, watching the recently choppy water begin to settle. The reddish color of blood begins to dissipate and the shark fins have vanished.

The metaphor for my job is obvious. On the surface, everything appears calm. However, just below the water, there is suffering and cruel death from sharks looking to feed on the helpless. I am contemplating why I took this job in the first place and recognize that failure is not an option.

# CHEAP DATES

**Location:** *My hotel room*
**Time:** *1300 hours*

After my eventful morning watching a man being eaten alive by sharks, I am back in my hotel room plotting how to save my own skin. If I don't succeed in my operation against Mr. David, that could just as easily be me—a chewed corpse sinking 500 meters to the bottom of the ocean.

I boot up my laptop and am greeted by some wonderful news—Mr. David has taken the bait. He has plugged the thumb drive into his computer. I now have full access into his files. The towel boy at the tennis club came through for me. Too bad he won't be able to collect on the other forty dollars I promised him. When, not if, I pull off this little caper, the king will forever be in my debt. I will have a lifetime membership to the Royal Tennis Club. On second thought, once I am done with this consulting engagement, I will never step foot in this shithole again.

Perusing Mr. David's files, I am disappointed that I am not finding the usual patterns of activity commonly typically concealed on a man's computer. I have yet to find porn. There are no emails from mistresses. No shady bank transfers. After two hours of searching, I am frustrated to discover that this man is relatively clean and ethical. No, I'm not looking hard enough. If there is one thing that I've learned over all these years of navigating the underworld of geopolitics, it is that every man has at least one skeleton in his closet. Since I skipped breakfast,

I order a club sandwich and Coke from room service to give me some energy. I cannot stop until I find what I am looking for. Four hours later, I do.

In two days Mr. David will be giving a speech in the country's third largest city. What's more important is that, because he is a "man of the people," he is going to be staying in a very simple hotel. This is my opportunity.

I Google the hotel where he will be staying and conduct my basic due diligence. The hotel website isn't bad and gives a decent overview of the property and rooms. I look at some overhead satellite imagery and study the roads leading in and out. I call the reception desk of the hotel and, using my unique social engineering skills, ask what appear to be very routine questions. The young lady on the other end of the phone is unwittingly giving me a ton of useful information to help destroy the next would-be leader of her country. It never ceases to amaze me how people who try to be helpful can do their organizations more harm than good. I'm sure the hotel's security director would be extremely suspicious if he were to overhear our conversation. But who am I kidding? This is a small hotel in Africa. Any problems I encounter can easily be swept under the rug with a few rolls of cash.

I work through the night to finalize my plan. The next morning I am up bright and early to travel to the new city. I do not let Amin know of my travels. This will no doubt upset him, but I cannot have interference from him or Mohammed. They would only draw needless attention should I request their assistance.

I walk six blocks from the hotel in the early morning light and find a taxi driver sitting in his car, reading a newspaper. He is a local African man in his early twenties.

Pretending not to have good English, I say to him, "Excuse . . . you speak English?"

"*Oui* . . . a little."

I explain to him that I need to travel to this other city but am too afraid to drive a car myself. I immediately see dollar signs in his eyes. He has found the dumb white tourist who he can substantially overcharge. We agree on a ridiculously expensive price, since I have to stick to my role as an inexperienced foreigner. I jump in the back of his beat up taxi, which is bad even by Africa standards.

The drive in the smelly, un-air-conditioned car takes us about two hours along a cracked asphalt highway. The view is mostly heavy bush in either direction. There are occasional baboons and other exotic wildlife in the trees. When we do pass other vehicles, they are mostly diesel Mercedes trucks hauling propane tanks or fruit. It is uncomfortably hot and we speak very little during the trip. I spend most of it hiding my face behind the newspaper. The driver just listens to the local news on the radio. Most of it has to deal with Mr. David's upcoming speech and how he could be the new leader of the country.

There is no road sign that indicates arrival into our destination city. We merely begin to encounter more evidence of civilization. First an auto parts shop, which is nothing more than a mud hut with rusted engine parts and spare tires scattered out in front of it, followed by one wooden fruit or Coca-Cola stand after another. This city is even poorer than the capital. Sickly thin people squat in the shade lining the muddy street. One would be hard-pressed to find a Wi-Fi signal, much less cell phone reception, in this part of the country. It dawns on me that the driver could easily kill me right now and leave me for dead, and no one would ever find my body.

As we grow closer to the main part of the city, I instruct the driver to drop me at the hotel. This is the same hotel that Mr. David will be staying in tomorrow night. The dilapidated building is a three-story remnant of the colonial days. It must have been built in the 1940s. Unfortunately, it doesn't appear to have been kept up much since then. I give the driver a one hundred dollar American bill. He smiles widely, exposing his stained yellow and brown teeth. I then instruct him to give me his name and cell phone number should I need him again. His name is François.

I pull out another Ben Franklin and hold it front of François' face. I tell him to drive back to the capital and wait for my call. If he promises to keep his mouth shut, and not mention that he drove a white man to this location today, I will give him this other $100. He gladly complies.

However, as I go to place the currency in his hand I quickly snatch it back and in an intimidating voice say, "François, I now know your name, your phone number, and your taxi. If you keep your mouth shut, I will continue to use your services and pay you good money. If you tell anyone about me, I will be sure that it is the worst decision you ever make. Do you understand what I am saying to you?"

François nods his head in compliance. A taxi driver in this part of the world knows full well how the game is played. Staying silent means repeat business. Talking means certain death. It is a simple negotiation. Plus, I only need François to keep his mouth shut for another few days until my plan is finished and I can vacate the country. I hand him the bill and he speeds away a happy man. He has just earned $200, enough to probably feed his family for six months.

I walk into the stuffy hotel only to find an empty lobby covered in dust. They must not get a lot of visitors. There is no doorman, but there is a teenage bellboy in a colorful African shirt that attempts to take my one carry-on suitcase. I may need his help later, so I let him take it from me. I ask an old man behind the reception desk, who most probably is the owner of this dive, if the best room is available for two nights. As I had hoped, he tells me that it is available tonight, but tomorrow it has already been reserved. That guest is obviously going to be Mr. David. I inform the old man that I would be happy to stay in that room tonight and then move in the morning to a lesser room, preferably on the same floor.

Without giving me a quizzical look or other indication of my suspicious behavior, the old man tells me that the room adjacent to the "suite" is available for both nights and is just as nice. I explain that I prefer to stay in the best room for just one night, and then will be happy to move first thing in the morning so housekeeping can have it nice and ready for the next guest. My luck then really improves. The old man tells me that it will be an easy move, as there is a door that connects the two rooms together. Bingo! Not only will I have one night in Mr. David's room ahead of time, I will also be in the adjoining room when he arrives. My plan just got that much easier.

The old man asks for a copy of my passport, to which I simply slide another one hundred dollar bill across the counter.

"My name is Benjamin Franklin. That should be enough identification."

The old man nods in acceptance and quickly collects the bill off the reception desk.

I am handed an old brass key and told my room number. The teenage bellboy leads the way with my rolling carry-on suitcase in tow. We ride up a creaky, tiny elevator, which barely accommodates the two of us, plus my suitcase. Stepping out of the rusty metal box, the boy leads me down a dank corridor to the hotel's executive suite. The carpets must have been red when the hotel was originally built, but are now brownish. I see no evidence of any CCTV cameras. Even if there were some, I doubt they would function. We finally reach the entry door at the end of the hall. I have reached ground zero. This is where my grand consulting operation will unfold, an operation that will ruin one man, keep another in power, and earn me a seven-figure paycheck.

I unlock the room door and the bellboy leads the way into the executive suite. *What a dump,* I think. Although the space is big, the carpet is filthy and the bed looks like it was bought used from an African whorehouse. The furniture is old and stained with some unrecognizable fluids, which I prefer not to know about. The window overlooks an impoverished shantytown. For my purposes, the room is perfect.

The bellboy gives me a brief tour of the amenities and educates me on how to use the air conditioning unit, which is nothing more than a loud aluminum box underneath the windowsill.

The boy then says the words to me that will set my plan in motion. "Sir, if there is anything you need at all, please don't hesitate to call me. My name is Dominique."

"Tell me, Dominique," I respond, "is it possible to get a girl to come up to my room and give me a massage?"

"Of course, sir. I can easily arrange for that."

"What about two girls?" I continue.

The teenager replies, "Sir, I can get you four girls. Any age you want."

I reach into my wallet, pull out a fifty-dollar bill and hand it to the boy.

"Dominique, tonight I want you to send two girls, around age twenty, up to my room at ten o'clock . . . for a massage. Do you understand?"

"No problem, sir."

"There is one catch, Dominique; you cannot tell anyone about this. Not even the manager at the desk. Can you do that?"

"Yes, sir. The owner leaves at eight each night. Then it is just me and the night manager on duty. It is easy to sneak the girls past him because he stays in the office and watches television."

"Good," I say. "It is important that only you, me, and the two girls know about the massage. Yes?"

"Of course, sir. I will bring them both up here at ten."

With that, the entrepreneurial bellboy disappears out the door and into the dark hallway.

I throw my suitcase on the bed and unzip it. Removing my clothes, I slide my fingers along the inside edges of the bag. I feel for a minor groove and pull up on it. A loud tearing of Velcro reveals a secret panel in the bottom of my bag. Concealed within the space are my special electronic gear, including several wireless covert cameras, a lock-picking set, and medical supplies.

It is time to perform an assessment on the room and set my trap for Mr. David.

I spend two hours setting the stage for his upcoming performance. I install the wireless pinhole cameras throughout the room. These mini devices, no larger than a coin, are covertly placed in the smoke alarm, air-conditioning vent, headboard of the bed, and desk. I also install one in the bathroom ceiling. I can monitor them remotely from my laptop in my room next door. I am halfway there with my preparations. Theoretically, these are my fishing poles. Now I just have to bait my hook. That will come in the form of the two girls.

I hear a knock at my door at around ten. I open it to find Dominique with his teenage arms around two slutty females. One is cute, around twenty years of age, and built like an Olympic sprinter. The other one looks to be in her late twenties, perhaps a big sister to the other one, and although fit, she is ugly as sin. Both are wearing red velvet mini-skirts with bright red lipstick and spike-heeled shoes. Not only do they look ridiculous they also look as if they could be carrying a plethora of venereal diseases.

They are exactly what I had hoped for.

I thank Dominique and tell him that he may go. He hurries away obediently. I invite the girls into the room and they head straight to the edge of the bed. They are both anxious to negotiate a price from this white man who must be wealthy, since he is staying in this "luxury" penthouse suite. I ask the girls if they would like a glass of Scotch. Their eyes light up and they both nod yes while smiling. *Very good*, I think. It is important that these girls are drinkers as well. Handing them their drinks, I inform them that although they will be getting well compensated this evening and, to their surprise, "no sex will be taking place." They look back at me and simply tell me that they will do whatever I request. This is excellent. For the next sixty minutes, I walk them through their role for the following evening.

The girls are under the impression that my very good friend Mr. David will be coming to the hotel tomorrow to celebrate his birthday. I am going to surprise him with these two sexy ladies as his present. All they have to do is dress in white clothes, knock on his door, and say that they are "complimentary massage girls," courtesy of the hotel for staying in the penthouse suite. They should then provide him with a glass of complimentary champagne, which I will have specially prepared with a date-rape drug, in order to help him relax. Once he falls asleep during his "massage," they should unlock the connecting door between our two rooms and let me in. It is all very straightforward.

Before they leave the room for the night, I hand each girl a wad of cash and instruct them that should they tell anybody at all about our plan that they will not be paid a thing tomorrow night. However, if they keep their mouths absolutely shut and not speak a word of the plan to anyone, they will be compensated with more money than they have ever seen. Discretion equals cash. In a poor country like this, I feel confident that the girls will not talk. It is now a waiting game until Mr. David arrives tomorrow morning. Both his reputation and mine are in jeopardy depending upon the outcome of the plan. We—and the citizens of this nation—are theoretically at the mercy of two cheap prostitutes.

# SHOW TIME

*Location:* *The Hotel Restaurant*
*Time:* *0830 hours*

I barely slept last night. I must have checked and re-checked the camera surveillance equipment thirty times. I then placed a lubricant from my shaving kit on the hinges of the inner door connecting the two rooms to eliminate any squeaking when I sneak into Mr. David's room. To calm my nerves I took a couple drinks of the Scotch to help me sleep. In the morning, I sat in the simple four-table restaurant of the hotel slugging down instant coffee. There was also a dirty glass of instant orange juice powder staring at me, which is making my stomach turn. My breakfast isn't much better—stale French bread with marmalade, two undercooked fried eggs, and a cup of spoiled yogurt. I opt to just eat the bread and drink the coffee. Of all the food laid out in front of me, those two items provide the least chance of giving me food poisoning. I can't afford to get sick right now.

After three cups of coffee, along with a banana that I talked the teenage waitress, who is probably the manager's granddaughter, into hunting down from the kitchen, I make my way back to my room. I need a hot shower. As I am walking through the tiny lobby I hear a car pull up the gravel driveway. I immediately feel a surge of adrenaline shoot through my body. I peer through the lobby window and my fear is confirmed—it's Mr. David. *What the fuck is he doing here so early?* I suddenly realize that my suitcase and clothes are in his soon-to-be Presidential Suite.

I have also set up a monitoring station in the adjoining room, which currently resembles something from a NASA control center. I need to get my things moved from the suite into the other room as quickly as possible.

Mr. David looks road weary from the drive and is dressed in a tan, wrinkled, safari suit. He also is sporting a pair of mirrored aviator sunglasses. Some things in Africa never change.

*Shit!* He cannot be allowed to recognize me! I must get up to my room and hide! I pick up the pace and head towards the staircase. I take the stairs two at a time back to my room. In my confused and dehydrated hung-over state, I miss a step and come crashing down on the stairwell landing. My hands and chest catch just as my forehead bounces off the concrete like a basketball. The pain is immense and I see stars. I try to hold in a muffled scream. This is not the time for self-pity. I pick myself up and keep moving.

Entering my hotel room door, I jump over the bed and make my way to the window. I am just in time see through the curtain and spot Mr. David standing behind a decades old, copper-colored, Mercedes four-door sedan, instructing his driver on which bags to collect from the trunk. Also with Mr. David are two more giant bodyguards. Each of them must be at least two meters tall and weigh well over 110 kilos. They both wear undersized black suits, which don't look to have been dry cleaned in weeks. For a country with so many hungry citizens, I apparently keep discovering bodyguards who seemed to have never missed a meal. A gun holster reveals itself when one of the bodyguards lifts a bag from the trunk. This man is packing a nickel-plated Smith and Wesson .45 caliber handgun. These two could be a problem; I was only planning on one bodyguard.

Suddenly, I see a fifth man emerge from the back of the Mercedes. He is about Mr. David's age, with bright white hair against his dark African skin, and appears to be more polished than the two muscle heads. His navy blue suit looks to have been bought in Europe. I guess he is a political adviser or campaign manager. Maybe my plan is not going to be as easy as I thought. A bead of salty sweat drips from my forehead and I curse myself under my breath for drinking too much the night before. No time to feel sorry for myself, I have an operation to conduct.

I open the door between the two rooms and quickly begin to throw my clothes from the Presidential Suite into the command center located in the room next door. The blaring loud ring of the telephone startles me. I calm my breathing and answer the receiver like a man in full control. It is the old man from the front desk asking me if I could please move out of the Presidential Suite, as tonight's VIPs have arrived early. *No shit,* I think.

I inform the old man that I am already packed and ready to move next door. He sounds relieved and tells me that a maid will be up in a few moments to clean the suite and provide me with the key. I pretend that I will be waiting for the maid to bring me the new room key. I simply request from the old man that the new guests wait before coming up, as I am embarrassed that I may have left the room a little messy and I don't want them to notice the person before them. The old man simply responds, "*Oui, monsieur.*"

After two minutes, the maid arrives with the key to the adjoining room. I hold an empty suitcase as she knocks on the door. She is ready to clean and I am not going to stand in her way. I retrieve the new key and disappear into the room located immediately next to this one. I breathe a sigh of relief, as I am now safe in my new room. I boot up the computer monitors and watch the maid as she prepares the Presidential Suite for Mr. David. I test the microphones and can easily hear her singing to herself while she changes the bed sheets. When she transitions into the bathroom I switch on that camera at my makeshift command post and listen as she complains to herself, in her native tribal language, about having to scrub the toilet. The devices are well hidden. Thank God all of the equipment is working.

Another twenty minutes and the room is ready. The maid walks to the phone next to the bed and calls down to the front desk. Informing the old man at the reception that the room is clean, she takes one last look around and exits the room. It's show time. I look at myself in the mirror above the desk in my room and notice that a swollen red lump has appeared on my forehead.

A few moments later, I hear Mr. David and his crew walking down the hallway. I peer out through the peephole on my door and see the curved shapes of four men directly on the opposite side. I watch as Mr. David inserts his key, while his adviser and two bodyguards look over his shoulder. One of the bodyguards suddenly turns to look at the peephole on my door.

*Shit! Can he see me? Am I leaving a shadow under the door?*

I freeze. After a few seconds that feel like hours, he looks away as if it were nothing. The four men enter the Presidential Suite. Trying to move as quietly as a cat, I spring on my tiptoes over to the electronic surveillance monitoring station.

"You two, wait outside," Mr. David orders the bodyguards in his eloquent French accent. The two giants comply without saying a word. They turn and head out into the hallway. I curse myself again for not installing a hidden camera in the hallway as well. Now I will have to rely solely on my peephole to be able to see them stand guard outside Mr. David's door, which unfortunately does not provide me with the best viewing angle.

Turning my attention back to the monitor, I see that Mr. David is now sitting on the bed, while his adviser is standing by the window.

The adviser speaks and I clearly pick up the conversation. "I'm glad we finally made it here. Your speech tomorrow will be the turning point of the election. You should focus on getting some good rest tonight."

"Don't I know it? My friend, I may appear on the surface as calm as a duck swimming across a pond, but underneath the water, my feet are churning nonstop. I don't know how much more of this stress I can take," responds David.

*I have just the thing to soothe your nerves, Mr. David. Two lovely young ladies will surprise you later this evening.*

"Why don't you take a nap now and then just stay in and order some room service tonight?" the adviser suggested.

"That's a good idea," Mr. David acknowledged. "Bringing about change through a free and fair election is never an easy task—particularly in this part of the world where corruption and evil are rampant. May my words tomorrow change this country for the better. God knows that these good people deserve more."

Mr. David's honest words bring me a twinge of guilt.

The adviser puts his hand on Mr. David's shoulder and tells him that he will be back in a few hours to wake him for lunch.

Afterwards, they will practice the speech together. David nods and the adviser exits the room. Returning to my peephole, I see the adviser move down the hallway with one of the bodyguards in tow. Hopefully, he is staying on another floor. The other security guard remains outside of the Presidential Suite. Like a sentry standing post, this mountain of a man is going to keep me trapped in my room. I wonder how many hours he is going to remain there. He can't stand all day. The other guard will probably come to relieve him at lunchtime. Well, at least I only have to contend with one man outside Mr. David's door and not two.

Per his adviser's nap suggestion, Mr. David takes a hot shower and then crawls into bed. Soon he is fast asleep. I use this opportunity to take a hot shower myself and review my plan once again. I feel that there is nothing more I can do for now, so I pull the curtains close and sit in the stained chair next to the window. I lean my thumping head back. I might as well grab a nap myself until Mr. David wakes up for lunch.

# CONDUCTING THE OPERATION

**Location:** *The Hotel Room*
**Time:** *2004 hours*

I dream of my childhood. I am twelve years old again and playing basketball with my father in the driveway of our simple home. Life then felt free and easy. How did I go from that upbringing to this crazy life I lead now? What if I had made one or two different decisions several decades ago? Would I still be doing this crazy job, living this crazy lifestyle? I am certain the answer is "no." More importantly, do I regret those decisions?

I awake to the sound of knocking and girls giggling. I open my eyes but everything is black. *Where the hell am I right now?* I take a deep breath and realize that I am still in the chair of my hotel room. Night has fallen. My head is still leaned back and I am staring straight at the ceiling in the dark. I pull my head down to my chin and I feel a twinge in my neck. It is completely stiff and has a painful kink on the right side. *What time is it?*

The monitors on the desk across from me are in sleep mode. I straighten up in the chair and tap the space bar on my computer keyboard. Three monitors suddenly come to life and flood the darkened room with a bright white light. The clock on the screen reads 10:04.

"Noooo!" I whisper.

I've been asleep for over nine hours. It is time for the operation to begin.

Focusing on the computer screens, I see that Mr. David is answering his hotel room door. The two girls have just knocked and are still standing in the hallway with one of the bodyguards giving them a suspicious stare.

"*Oui?*" asks Mr. David.

His bodyguard informs him that these two girls have been sent up with compliments of the hotel manager to provide him with a massage and a basket of fruit and champagne. He says it is included with all guests who stay in the Presidential Suite.

I bite my bottom lip and pray that Mr. David accepts the bait.

"Certainly, come in, ladies."

*Yes, let the games begin.*

Mr. David leads the two young women into his room. The ugly one begins to take charge. She informs him to lie on the bed in his boxer shorts, while the other girl opens the bottle of champagne for the three of them to enjoy together. Mr. David quickly complies by sliding off his shirt and pants and sitting upright on the side of the bed.

Politicians are such easy prey.

I am amazed at how naturally the girls slip into their roles and carry out their assignments. Perhaps I shouldn't be surprised. These are working girls in a third-world country, where the average person earns a few dollars per day. This is the only way they know how to survive.

While Mr. David is taking direction from the ugly prostitute, the more attractive girl discreetly reaches into her purse for one of the knockout drugs. Through the monitors I see her crush a pill into a powder. She then slips it into his glass of champagne like a professional magician performing a sleight-of-hand trick. The three of them have a toast to Mr. David's speech tomorrow, and within a few seconds, his glass is empty. I'm smiling.

A few minutes later, Mr. David is face down on the bed with his arms and legs spread. The two girls are topless and on their knees above him, rubbing his shoulders and hamstrings with some lotion they found in the bathroom. It is obvious to me that the sleeping pills were not necessary. In fact, they are now probably counterproductive, as I have a strong suspicion that Mr. David would freely have had sex with the girls—which would have made for a more compelling video. I can see a corner of a smile from Mr. David's face, which is buried in a pillow. I imagine he is thinking that this will be a nightly event when he becomes the next president of this tiny nation. Soon, however, that smile relaxes as he slips into a drug-induced stupor. He begins to snore loudly. Now it's my turn.

I move up from my monitoring station to the connecting door in my room. I open it and knock twice softly on the other one. The attractive girl dutifully opens it. The two prostitutes stand before me topless and smiling ear to ear. They are so proud of their work and recognize that they are going to earn a big payday.

But our work is not done. I pop back in my room for just a second to grab my camera. We must now take pictures of Mr. David in all sorts of compromising and certainly unflattering positions.

For the next twenty minutes, the girls straddle, twist, squeeze, insert, and kiss Mr. David's naked body, and perform several other, more disgusting sexual acts using erotic toys. Like a professional photographer, I quietly direct the girls' performance. The key is to make it look as though Mr. David is actually awake and enjoying these acts. I also shoot several videos so that no one can claim the pictures have been altered. Although the girls are having fun, I am all business. It is much harder than you can imagine to make a lifeless person appear to be enjoying a threesome on film.

A loud knock on the door suddenly interrupts the moment.

"Sir, it's Michael. Is everything all right in there?"

*Shit. It is Mr. David's campaign manager. The bodyguard must have informed him of the two girls.*

Thinking quickly, I call out a nervous, *"Oui."*

"Sir, please open the door. I would like to speak with you for a moment"

*Dammit!* I can probably fool this guy with a one-word answer, but I shouldn't try to say anything else. Thinking fast, I instruct the pretty girl to get under the covers with Mr. David. I next tell the ugly one to answer the door and tell the man and his comrades that Mr. David is busy with her friend and that he should come back in the morning. Then I quickly return to my room and watch through the monitors.

*This could be the end of me,* I think. If the men barge in it won't take them but a minute to realize that someone else probably entered through the adjoining hotel room door. I go to the window and quietly slide it open. If I have to, I can jump three stories to the ground below. But then what? I will have to make my way by foot into the town to find a taxi. No. I have been in worse situations than this before. This will be fine.

I watch as the ugly girl opens the door for Mr. David's campaign manager.

"Where is Mr. David?" he sternly asks, with the bodyguard attempting to peer in over his shoulder.

"In bed with my girlfriend," she replies.

"David! David! Are you alright?" the man calls into the room. *Shit!* I'm finished.

"He can't talk right now," the girl says smiling as she smartly blocks the doorway.

"Why?" the man demands.

Looking him straight in the eyes and with a harsh, irritable tone, the clever girl replies, "Because my girlfriend is sitting on his face right now and his mouth is busy doing something else. In fact, my mouth is supposed to be doing something else instead of talking to you. Mr. David says that you need to mind your own business and come back in the morning."

"Okay, okay," the manager replied. "Calm down. I will come back in the morning."

Before closing the door, the girl says one more thing that demonstrates her impressive street smarts.

"What room are you staying in? My girlfriend and I will come visit you when we're done here."

The campaign manager suddenly softens his demeanor and breaks into a smile. "Room 202. Yes, please come visit me when you have concluded your business with Mr. David."

The manager departs and the girl locks the door. She walks over to the interior door and lets me in. I tell her that she has done an outstanding job and is worthy of a nice tip. She is already aware that she is going to make more money tonight than she will all year.

We conclude our operation with the still unconscious Mr. David flat on his back. He'll awake in the morning with no memory of what happened. He will just think he got a massage and then passed out. I tidy up all the incriminating evidence, which includes the colorful sex toys. I give them to the girls as a keepsake.

I hand each girl five one-hundred-dollar bills. I instruct them never to speak a word of what happened tonight. I don't try and threaten them, because even if they did talk, no one would believe them and they would only end up hurting themselves in the long run.

I disappear into my room through the adjoining door, while the girls exit Mr. David's room. Standing at the peephole of my door, I hear the ugly prostitute—the one who saved my ass tonight—tell the bodyguard standing post, "Mr. David says he does not want to be disturbed until the morning." *Damn, she's good!*

The bodyguard nods to the girl as if she is his superior giving a direct order. The girl then tells him that he shouldn't waste his time standing outside the door. The bodyguard agrees and walks down the hallway with the girls under each arm. It seems these ladies have a lot more money to make tonight.

It is in my best interest to gather up my equipment and get out of town. I call down to the bellboy and instruct him to have a reliable taxi—fully fueled for a long trip—waiting for me in front of the hotel in ten minutes. I then make my way down the stairwell with my luggage, careful to avoid being seen or heard by anyone. I reach the lobby to find the bellboy waiting for me alone by the reception desk. My taxi has already arrived. I hand the boy four hundred-dollar bills and tell him it's for the cost of my room. I then hand him four more and remind him that I was never there.

Five minutes later, I sit in the back of the taxi, an old man behind the wheel, driving me back toward the capital. My job in this country is done. There is a flight to Europe that leaves in exactly six hours. I already have a first-class seat reserved.

# SHEIKS
## II

# DOWN TIME

**Location:** *Lake Como, Italy*
**Time:** *0726 hours*

It is a beautiful spring morning as I sit at a tiny round bistro table on the wrought-iron balcony of my 400-year-old rented villa in the hills overlooking Lake Como. I have been coming to this serene section of Northern Italy for over two decades, typically to unwind after my more strenuous consulting engagements. The picturesque, snowcapped mountains, reflecting in the serene lake below, calm my nerves and allow me to forget about the constant state of vigilance that I'm required to maintain while on assignment.

I'm enjoying a double espresso in my Turkish cotton bathrobe, while leisurely flipping through the pages of the *Financial Times*. I look back into the bedroom to see that my date from last night, a strikingly attractive Italian woman in her mid-thirties, is still asleep naked in my bed. For years, this equally successful international beauty and I have occasionally met up in different parts of the globe to share dinner and swap stories, among other things. Last night we spent three hours experiencing a culinary masterpiece of lamb chops and risotto in the private dining room of Il Gatto Nero restaurant in the hills of Cernobbio. Famous resident George Clooney was also known to regularly reserve this small room, with an amazing view of Lago di Como, whenever he wanted to impress his latest supermodel or Hollywood starlet girlfriend. That gets me to thinking; *if George Clooney can eventually settle down with one woman, maybe it's time for me to do the same.* Still staring at this lovely, olive-skinned brunette in my bed, I wonder if she and I are eventually supposed to be married. Maybe we will have three small kids and a golden retriever, live in a two-story brick house in the suburbs, and drive our SUV to Disney World during the holiday season. The thought makes me laugh and I return to my newspaper.

It's been almost three weeks since I snuck out of Africa in the early morning hours. A lot has happened since then. When I returned to Europe, I sent Mr. David a few samples of the incriminating photos from an anonymous email address. I essentially told him that unless he dropped out of the presidential race and threw his support behind the king, these photos and several others—plus videos—would not only go out to his wife, supporters, and church members, but would also be sent to international media networks such as CNN, BBC, as well as all the international newspapers. However, if he did comply with this demand, he would be rewarded with an ambassadorship to one of the lovely island nations off the coast of Africa—perhaps even the Seychelles. It was an easy, albeit painful, decision for him. It also allowed the king to control and keep tabs on his future activities. Like Vito Corleone, *I made him an offer he couldn't refuse.*

As for me, Mohammed actually lived up to his end of the bargain. Once Mr. David officially bowed out of the presidential race and publically pronounced that the king should be "leader for life," three million euros were deposited into my account in Switzerland. For a while I thought that he might try to stiff me out of payment. However, both Mohammed and the king were smart enough to know that if I could deliver results this fast, they would be smart to keep me happy in case they needed my services once more in the future. Although I never plan to enter their country again, they could be a good referral for future business. Let's face it, men like Mohammed and the king have equally needy friends who are also willing to pay top dollar to make their headaches go away. But enough about business. Right now I just want to take it easy and decide on how I want to spend my money.

After another session in bed, followed by breakfast on the balcony, I kiss my friend goodbye. I watch her as she drives away in her red Alfa Romeo convertible, her dark Italian hair blowing in the wind. Who knows how long it will be before we see each other again—if ever? She disappears out of my sight, heading down the hillsides of Como.

After a long, hot shower in my marble-enclosed bathroom, I decide to take the train into Milan to have another suit made. It is time to visit with my tailor Enzo at the Brioni store located across from the Four Seasons, where I once witnessed Sophia Loren step out of a white Rolls Royce in an equally blazing white fur coat, while I was being fitted. I will also make it a point to stop by Luini Panzerotti, located near Milano's famous Duomo, for a fried panzerotti, essentially the most delicious pizza snack in all of Italy.

I'm sipping a glass of prosecco from a crystal flute, as Enzo lays a sampling of silk neckties out before me to match the suit I was just fitted for. One is a checkered white and red, while the others are a stripped blue and solid blue. Each tie costs three-hundred euros. He smiles when I say that I will take them all. My cell phone begins to vibrate. Very few people have this number and it may go weeks without activity. Therefore, I immediately know that it signifies a new consulting opportunity.

"Yes," I simply say into the phone.

"Yes, sir. I was told that if I called this number I would be able to speak to a consultant," says the deep accented voice on the other end of the line.

"I am the consultant. May I ask who gave you this number?"

"Of course. It was Yousef Azzam in Riyadh."

I immediately recognize the name. He is a wealthy businessman in Saudi Arabia who previously served in the Saudi Ministry of Interior as an intelligence officer. Yousef and I have been friends for over a decade and I helped him import sensitive radar technology into the kingdom, bypassing international trade regulations. He made millions off the deal and became a nonstop referral machine for my practice. This was sure to be another lucrative engagement.

"Ah yes, Mr. Azzam. How is he these days?"

"He is very well," says the voice. "He tells me that you are the man I should speak to regarding assistance in acquiring some information."

"That depends upon the information you are in need of."

"I understand. Why don't we meet the day after tomorrow in Dubai? Say the lobby of the Burj al Arab Hotel at noon to discuss the particulars?"

"I'm sure Mr. Azzam has told you that I am a rather busy man and that my services do not come cheap."

"You need not worry about money, my friend. You will be adequately compensated merely for taking a meeting with me. Just be in the lobby of the Burj in two days at noon sharp. I promise that it will be worth your while."

"Very well," I reply.

"Excellent. I will be very easy to spot. I will be the large Arab man wearing a white *thawb*, the traditional long robe. My name is Sheik Omar al-Gaylani. See you then."

"I'm looking forward to it," I say.

Sheik Omar Gaylani. I know of this man. He is the owner of many telecom companies throughout the Middle East. He is easily worth billions. He is also someone you don't want to offend, as he has a nasty reputation as a vindictive bully. He makes Vladimir Putin look like a frightened wimp.

I tell Enzo that I that I'm not sure when I will be able to come back and collect my new suit. Therefore, he should just keep it on hold for me. Enzo is used to this from me. He tells me that it is no trouble at all, since I am one of his most loyal customers. I hand him 5,000 euros in cash and walk out into the bustling streets of Milano. I need to grab the train back to Lake Como to pack a suitcase. This evening I must fly to Dubai to meet a sheik.

# BUSINESS CLASS

**Location:** *Aboard Turkish Airways*
**Time:** *2330 hours*

I travel in business class to Dubai on an airline I don't typically use. It's important that I vary airlines to avoid a pattern. Enemies could easily learn whether I am enrolled in a frequent flier program, which could assist them in tracking my movements. I have an American diplomat sitting next to me on the plane. I spotted his black passport when he sat down and we struck up a mundane conversation about the weather. As I'm traveling on my Italian passport, I am careful not to reveal too much information about myself. Although the chances are remote, he could be working with the American CIA or FBI. When he asks me what I do, I simply tell him that I work for a private investment group that specializes in distressed assets. That comment seems to bore him into putting on his headphones and watching a video.

Typical government bureaucrat: one simple business term and he is lost. It seems that no matter what country you live in, the best and brightest never work for the government. Those individuals usually start enterprises that change the world. I laugh at the thought of Steve Jobs or Bill Gates trapped in a government cubicle in a civil servant job doing the bare minimum. My mind is now more at ease. It has always been my belief that the US Department of State only exists to provide cover for CIA officers working overseas and to issue visas to foreigners. This guy obviously does the latter. *Poor fellow.*

I am on my fourth glass of Argentinian Malbec, yet instead of relaxing I am becoming more restless. The man that I will meet in thirty-six hours is unlike the last buffoon I dealt with. I always like to be smarter than my clients. This next job may not be as easy.

\* \* \*

Sheik Omar al-Gaylani was born into a wealthy Saudi family that made its fortune in laying the original telephone lines in the kingdom, when the Americans and British first discovered oil in the desert back in the 1930s. Unlike most Saudi elites, his family originally came from Yemen and over time ascended to wealthier and wealthier rungs along the social ladder. Interestingly enough, Osama bin Laden's family also began with similar origins from Yemen. However, they made their money in construction, primarily of roads and mosques. Aside from the major "black sheep" in their family, Osama, the bin Laden name remains one of the most respected construction companies throughout the Middle East, a fact that I'm sure troubles most Americans. There's a running joke that the name "bin Laden" is as recognizable in the Saudi construction world as the name "Trump" is in the United States.

The sheik is now the patriarch of the al-Gaylani family, and has branched out from telephone lines into cell phone towers. In fact, the majority of the communications that occurs within in the kingdom must pass through his network. He's worth billions, although it still is just a fraction of the Saudi Royal family's wealth from oil revenues. Despite the financial discrepancy between the sheik and the king, it is safe to say that without his assistance in controlling all the airwaves, the Saudi Royal family would be helpless. Therefore, he garners much respect from the monarchy.

I ponder why the sheik requires my services. He mentioned that he needed me to provide him with some information. Could that mean he wants me to find a person for him? Perhaps it means that I need to get some dirt on a competitor? Maybe one of his sons has gotten himself into a legal mess and needs a "fixer" to make the problem disappear. Whatever it is, it must be important enough that the sheik himself is calling my cell phone.

A Turkish male flight attendant pushes a cart full of cheeses and aperitifs down the aisle and stops alongside of me. I opt for a plate of Brie and seasonal grapes but pass on the offer of a brandy snifter filled with cognac. I decided to go easy on the hard liquor and just stick to wine.

My American seatmate is fully engaged with an episode of the Simpsons. While he laughs out loud at Homer's antics, I laugh inside at the idea of this clown working as a covert operative. He is probably just another civil servant charged with some bullshit international outreach program, a "do-gooder" who could never make it in the private sector where success is gauged by one's ability to compete in business and relentlessly deliver results. Flying business class is another fine example of how American taxpayer dollars are wasted. In twenty years he will probably be retired and living on his meager government pension in a gated community in Florida.

After the flight attendant clears the empty wine glass and cheese plate from my tray table, I recline. I might as well try to relax and grab a nap. I put on my headphones and tune to the music channel. I select The Essential Dean Martin playlist and close my eyes while Dino sings *Volare*. The idiot next to me is still laughing hysterically at the Simpsons, as I slip into a dream.

# TO ARMS

*Location: Burj al-Arab Hotel, Dubai*
*Time: 1201 hours*

The Burj al-Arab is an icon in the Middle East. Shaped in the form of a towering glass ship with its sails filled with gusting winds, it was one of the original landmarks when Dubai was transitioning from a sleepy little outpost in the desert into a top international tourist destination and financial hub. It now serves as one of the finest hotels in the world, the first to be rated seven stars—out of a possible five. It sits on its own mini-island off the coast of Dubai in the Arabian Gulf (or Persian Gulf, depending upon who you are having dinner with). It is the place to see and be seen when visiting the United Arab Emirates. Interestingly enough, when the hotel was first being constructed, the mast for the ship's main sail of the structure was the first thing to be erected. As an ironic result, the metal spine of the building gave the appearance of a huge Christian crucifix towering over the predominantly Muslim country. Rumor has it that the Emir demanded that the builders work around the clock until the visual representation of a cross was concealed.

Breaking my usual protocol of not staying in the same hotel in which I take a meeting, I have booked a suite overlooking the water. My room is opulence taken to the extreme. The color scheme throughout the room is a royal blue and gold. Everything is of the finest quality—silk linens, gold trimmings, and mahogany wood finish. The marble bathroom is enormous and must have easily cost thirty thousand alone to construct. Although staying at the Burj may expose me to clandestine surveillance from the sheik's security detail, I feel confident that my old friend Yousef wouldn't allow me to be set up. Besides, I very much enjoy the creature comforts of the world's finest hotel.

\* \* \*

At seven forty-five the next night, I am sitting in the opulent lobby of the hotel sipping Perrier water with lime, when I easily spot the sheik. He is a mountain of a man. Although he is no more than six feet tall, he must easily weigh over 350 pounds. An older gentleman of sixty-two, it is obvious that his slicked-back hair and manicured goatee have both been dyed black. I'm not sure if he thinks this makes him look younger but it certainly makes him appear more maniacal and intimidating. He appears to be alone. However, men with his level of power are seldom alone. I am certain that he has his security team discreetly nearby.

As promised, he is wearing a bright white thwab, with matching kafia (headdress), which hangs off him like a bleached bed sheet. His fat, hairy feet are encased in tightly snug leather sandals and they remind me of hot bread rising in a bread pan. A gaudy gold watch, encrusted with diamonds around the bezel, hangs from his left wrist like a hunk of metal. On his opposite wrist is an equally thick gold bracelet. As he extends his hand to me for an introduction, I see what appears to be an American football Super Bowl ring on his ring finger.

"Hello. You must be the consultant. I am Mr. Gaylani," he says in a surprisingly cheerful voice.

"Pleasure to meet you, sir. My name is Noah."

"Mr. Noah. What a wonderful name. Is that your real name?"

"No."

"Interesting. So tell me, why do you choose this name to meet with me? Is it because you are a religious man?" asks the Sheik.

"Because Noah believed in preparation. I, like him, prefer to think that I have planned out everything ahead of time. That is essential for a man in my line of work."

This is a standard bullshit answer that I have always given to that question for years.

The sheik's laugh echoes throughout the sprawling lobby attracting the attention of other guests and the hotel staff. The sheik seems not to care and neither does anyone else.

"How wonderful! I like you already, Mr. Noah!" he continues to beam. I think that I have found the right man for the job."

"And what job is that, sir?" I ask.

"Ahh, one that will make both of us a lot of money," he sheepishly replies. "Come with me up to my room and we will discuss this in greater length over a drink."

I suddenly have a bad feeling in my gut. I make it a point never to meet someone on his or her turf, especially in his hotel room. However, because of this man's stature in the Gulf, it is best that I simply comply.

"Why not?" I say. "But first I must ask, is that an NFL Super Bowl ring on your finger?"

"Why, yes it is," beams the proud sheik. "It is from the last Super Bowl that the Dallas Cowboys won. My good friend, Jerry Jones (the owner of the team) had it made for me. I am very proud of it!"

This is getting better by the minute.

We move across the lobby to the bank of elevators. As the doors open to the lift, two hulking men in black suits—the official color of security—flank either side of us. They appear to be British, Australian, or South African. These must be the sheik's bodyguards. They are not going to allow the sheik to ride alone in the elevator with a stranger for fear that I could injure him, or worse. These guys are good. It reinforces the notion that I am not dealing with amateurs.

The elevator continues and reaches the top floor. The sheik has rented the entire penthouse. The elevator doors open directly into his two-story Royale Suite. At 8,500 square feet, it dwarfs my room. I think I read in an airplane magazine once that this suite costs $20,000 per night and ranks as one of the most exclusive rooms on the planet. I am dumbfounded by the luxury of it all and am now somewhat glad that I accepted the sheik's offer for that drink.

A butler dressed in a tuxedo greets us and asks if he can get us anything. I order a Johnny Walker Blue on the rocks.

So much for me not drinking hard liquor. The sheik requests a Dom Perignon with fresh strawberry juice. The security guards separate to opposite sides of the room and stand against the walls like disciplined sentries. These two are obviously privy to sensitive conversations and it strikes me how valuable it would be for a foreign intelligence service to recruit one of these guys to spy on the sheik for them. I hope that hasn't happened yet. Otherwise, I may have just exposed myself to the authorities.

"Come, sit down," says the sheik.

We move into the living room with large picture windows with a panorama overlooking the bright blue waters of the Gulf. On a massive white leather sofa are two voluptuous blonde girls in their twenties watching a rerun of the television show *Friends* on the largest flat-screen TV I've ever seen. They appear to be Scandinavian—judging by their accents they are either Swedish or Danish. They are wearing matching blue bikinis with silk tropical wraps around their waists and sandals on their feet. Stunning is the only word that can describe their beauty.

The sheik waves his hands as if he is shooing a cat off the furniture, and the two girls quickly move from the couch to the bedroom. Not a word is exchanged and the expression on the girls' faces is definitely one of annoyance. I wonder how much the sheik is paying these two to sleep with his fat ass. For their sake, I hope it is at least a six-figure sum. The sheik turns off the television with the universal remote that controls virtually everything from the lights to the curtains in the suite. The butler brings our cocktails on a silver serving tray and sets them down on the expensive wood coffee table in front of us. I thank the butler but the sheik does not bother.

"Now, Mr. Noah, let's discuss business."

"Of course."

"I was told by General Yousef that you are a man that can get things done. Is that correct?"

"It is."

"Excellent! Then I have a job for you."

I sit calmly as he continues.

"As you know, the security situation in Afghanistan is rather abhorrent. Since the Americans have officially pulled their troops out, all the innocent Muslims who supported the coalition—and a more civilized and peaceful way of life—have been slaughtered by the brutal, resurgent Taliban regime. I am afraid that all of the hard work, billions of dollars spent, and lives lost over the past decade will be for nothing if the Taliban is able to take control of the entire country once again. I, as a loyal servant of Allah, cannot in good conscience allow this to happen. *We*, Mr. Noah, cannot allow this happen. Therefore, in order to help the innocent Muslims protect themselves, we must arm the local tribes with weapons so that they can protect themselves from the invading Taliban attackers."

"Sheik," I begin, "with all due respect to you and all those needlessly suffering in Afghanistan, isn't this a job more suited for the international community rather than a lone man such as yourself? I mean, this is something that the coalition, the United Nations, the Gulf Cooperation Council (GCC), and all these other organizations should already be doing. Right?"

"*Should,* being the operative word, Mr. Noah. Allow me to explain. Since the time of Alexander the Great, Afghanistan has been more than a pile of rocks in Central Asia. Afghanistan's significance is that it simply cannot be tamed. Afghanistan is like a beautiful woman that every man wants but cannot have. A seductress. When she ignores their advances, men want her even more, and inevitably they will try to take her. The British learned this, as did the Soviets. Unfortunately, now too, have the Americans. Apparently, the Chinese will be the next to learn this painful lesson the hard way. And just like a woman, Afghanistan holds a secret. You see, she actually wants to you to try and take her. This is how she springs her trap. She feeds off the men who pump money and resources into her borders. She pretends that it will make things better; all the while she is playing both sides of the fence, disrupting progress and impeding development so that even more money and resources become necessary. Unfortunately, her cruel game brings with it death."

"Forgive me, sheik. If you are admitting that the situation in Afghanistan is essentially hopeless, won't it be counterproductive to inject even more weapons into the country?"

"Mr. Noah, I am disappointed. I thought you were smarter than that. Winning in Afghanistan is not my objective. Winning in Afghanistan is impossible. Making money in Afghanistan, on the other hand, is what I am after. Right now, there are more guns than people in Afghanistan—and goats for that matter. It is the one thing the country cannot get enough of. Surprisingly, cash is also readily abundant. All of these warlords have millions of dollars stashed away in bank accounts throughout the UAE and Switzerland—much of it given to them by foreign benefactors trying to garner their support. But guns are the real currency in Afghanistan. The warlord with the most guns wins. It is that simple. And it is our job is to fill that demand. If the Taliban are allowed to take over the country again completely, the demand will fall. Therefore, we must keep the chaos in just the proper balance. Guns keep this balance in check.

"I understand." (I lie.) "What is it you need me to do?"

"You will go to Beirut and meet with Yuri Berezovsky, a Russian arms dealer who helped get Putin elected. There he will escort you to Turkmenistan, where you will take delivery of a cargo plan full of AK-47 assault rifles, rocket-propelled grenade launchers (RPGs) and enough ammunition to invade Kuwait. You will fly with this plane into the Federally Administered Territory of Afghanistan—otherwise known as the FATA—and deliver these weapons to Whalid bin Talibani, the country's next great warlord. The entire job should take you two weeks. You will be compensated with two million US dollars."

"Why do you need me to do it? Why can't Yuri deliver these weapons for you himself?"

"Because I do not trust Russians," he says candidly. "I need someone whom I can trust to ensure that my shipment is not compromised. Yousef trusts you, which means that I trust you. You simply need to babysit the weapons while they are in transit to make sure that they reach their final destination. For this I will give you two million dollars—one million now and one million upon delivery. Do we have a deal?"

I sit quietly on the couch for a moment thinking to myself. This is suicide. I know a bad deal when I hear one.

"Mr. Noah, do we have a deal?"

I pause a moment and then say, "Five million."

"You insult me, Mr. Noah!"

"Your offer insults me, sir!"

The sheik smiles and bursts into his booming laugh again.

"Now I see why Yousef thinks so highly of you. None of my men would ever challenge what I offer them. You are different. Very well, Mr. Noah. You win. Five million dollars it is. Besides, I already have a helicopter waiting outside to take you to the airport, so I guess I have no choice."

I look out the picture window to see a black jet helicopter, with tinted black windows, hovering in the distance, its single large blade whirling and thumping.

"Gather your belongings and meet the helicopter on the helipad," the sheik instructs me. "It will take you to the airport where my private jet will fly you to Beirut. Check into Le Gray Hotel and wait for Yuri to contact you. To verify his identity, he will have a newspaper in his left hand when he first greets you. If he does not, it means that it is not him."

With that, we both get up from the couch and the sheik extends his fat hand to me once more.

"Good luck, Mr. Noah."

"Thank you, sir."

The sheik smiles, turns, and walks towards his bedroom. As the door closes behind him I see the two blonde girls lying on the oversized bed. I don't know whom I feel more sorry for at the moment—them or me.

# FLYING SOLO

*Location: Burj al-Arab Hotel*
*Time: 2205 hours*

I hustle down to my room and gather my belongings. Luckily, I have always made it a point to have my luggage pre-packed at all times. Within two minutes I am ready to depart. I notify the lovely young lady sitting at the reception desk located at the end of my floor's hallway—for at the Burj al-Arab Hotel every floor has its own concierge desk—that I am checking out and to just charge everything to my credit card on file. I make a mental note to destroy that credit card after this trip and to never use this particular identity again.

I take the elevator up to the HELIPAD level. Sitting 650 feet up, the circular helipad of the Burj is as recognizable as the hotel itself. It was on this pad that Roger Federer and Andre Agassi played a friendly tennis match, Tiger Woods smacked golf balls into the desert below, and a Formula One racecar burned its tires performing a death-defying spinning stunt. Right now, however, the pad is fulfilling its primary role as landing zone for my air taxi.

I board the sleek, black jet copter and strap in tight to one of the tan Corinthian leather seats. Almost immediately, the cool Arab pilot, sporting a three-day beard stubble and leather bomber jacket, quickly takes us high into the dark desert sky. Below us the city of Dubai is lit up brighter than the Las Vegas strip. We take off quickly, and within ten minutes are descending upon the private airfield at Dubai International Airport.

The wheels of the helicopter touch down and the pilot gives me the thumbs up. The door opens and I am greeted by yet another oafish–looking bodyguard who points across the tarmac to a white Gulfstream V jet parked just a few hundred feet away. It is the sheik's private jet, and it is easily worth $40 million. I quickly make my way towards it as if I own it.

I've flown on plenty of private jets before, but this one is by far the most impressive. The runway lights reflecting off the shiny wax on the fuselage seem to make the white paint sparkle in the darkness. The cabin door is open and the stairs leading into the plane are adorned with a blood red carpet. At the top of the steps is a curvaceous Swedish-looking woman in a neatly pressed navy blue suit. Her bleached blond hair is tied up tight in a bun under a small cap. As I get closer to her, I noticed that her skin is flawless. She must be around thirty-five, but she could easily pass for ten years younger. I conclude that the sheik definitely has a proclivity for bouncy blondes.

"*Guten tag.* I am Eva. Welcome aboard Mr. Gaylani's plane."

"*Guten tag,* Eva. It's a pleasure to make your acquaintance."

*Ah! So she's German and not Swedish.* Close enough. She's still ridiculously attractive. I'm going to enjoy this flight even more.

Eva invites me on board and gives me a quick tour of the cabin. Each of the eight swivel seats is made of the finest handcrafted Italian leather. Chestnut wood trim runs along the interior. Flat screen monitors are everywhere. The white shag carpet is what the ultra-rich call walking-around money, meaning they are so rich that they can pull off having a white shag carpet on a private jet. The bathroom is made up entirely of polished gold. Eva shows me into the oversized bedroom with its more than accommodating bed. My mind immediately begins to wonder if she and the sheik have been in there together before, while airborne.

"Can I get you a drink before takeoff?" she asks.

"It depends, will you have a drink with me?" I reply.

She smirks disapprovingly and explains that she is not allowed to drink while on duty. How very German of her.

I act disappointed—which I am—and tell her that I would

like a bourbon on the rocks.

Like a Bavarian robot, Eva mechanically hurries into the galley to prepare my drink. She must have done this a hundred times before. When she returns, she instructs me to fasten my seat belt, as we'll be airborne shortly. She then disappears into the cockpit. I determine that she probably sees me as just the next jerk, in a long line of jerks, to fly on her boss's jet. Hell, she's probably up there giving hand jobs to both the pilot and co-pilot right now. I don't need a woman like that. What's the matter with me? I'm already getting jealous—and I haven't even started drinking yet.

Twenty minutes after takeoff, Eva reemerges from behind the cockpit door and asks if I need a refill.

"Why not?" I say, shaking the cubes in the glass in front of her.

She refreshes my drink and says to me in her strict German accent, "What else can I do for you?"

"What else is there?" I ask.

"I could suck your dick if you'd like."

I nearly spit out my drink.

"Excuse me?" I say, startled. Did I just hear this beautiful woman correctly?

With a straight face and stern voice she boldly states, "I give a great blowjob. Would you like one?"

"What if one of the pilots comes out and sees us?" I stupidly ask.

"The plane is on autopilot," she calmly explains.

"Autopilot?" I say

"Yes, autopilot."

At this point, Eva kneels down before me and undoes my seat belt.

"Wait, where the fuck are the pilots?"

"I am the pilot," she says, unzipping my trousers.

"Hold on. You're the pilot? It's just you and me on this plane right now?

"Yes, darling. Now shut up and relax."

I try, but I take her hands in mine, stopping her. "What if another airplane is flying in the same airspace?"

"What are you a homo or something?" she barks.

"No. But to be honest, I wouldn't mind knowing Sully Sullenburger was sitting at the controls right now."

"Who?"

I look down at this lovely, healthy woman kneeling between my legs. Eva's beautiful face is shooting me an inquisitive look. She is absolutely gorgeous, and I suddenly forget about the possibility of a midair collision.

Just as she starts pulling down my boxer shorts, my training and experience kicks in. This is a total set-up by the sheik. I grab Eva's strong shoulders and push her back before she can seduce me any further.

"I'm sorry, Eva," I say in a less-than-apologetic voice. "You are incredibly attractive, but I cannot do this right now. I have to concentrate on my business."

Eva stands up without saying a word and walks back to the galley. I can tell she is humiliated. I lean back in my luxurious chair and look up at the ceiling. There are ridiculous neon blue lights up there, which slowly fade in and out, I assume in an attempt to provide some kind of calming effect. I am also certain that the sheik has plenty of hidden cameras installed up there, as well. There's no doubt that he—and Eva—have captured many frequent fliers on video. The purpose of the evidence could be blackmail or some other perverted reason (maybe the sheik just likes to watch!) The French Intelligence Service has repeatedly been rumored to have installed audio and video devices in the business class cabin of Air France flights for decades. Their intention was to overhear and identify targets of opportunity for economic espionage collection. Apparently, the sheik has taken things one step further on his own aircraft.

I take a moment to reflect. *Damn, who am I? What am I doing here?*

I look over and see that my drink hasn't spilled. This must be my lucky day. I slam back the glass of bourbon and walk up towards the galley. Eva isn't there. She must have gone back into the cockpit. I get the impression that I won't see her again until we land. I decide to pour myself another drink.

I plunk back down into my seat and put the noise-canceling headphones, connected within the armrest, over my ears. Ironically, the '80s hit, "I Want Your Sex," by the late George

Michael, is playing. Now I am certain that Eva's proposition was a set up. I pat myself on the back for my intuition. However, before I give myself too much credit, I remember that I—like millions of other people—thought that George Michael was once straight. Maybe I'm not the infallible judge of character I thought I was. Soon thereafter I drift off to sleep.

* * *

I awake to Eva's voice over the intercom system.

"We will be landing in ten minutes, please fasten your seat beat."

Her announcement sounds as if she is addressing a group of elderly passengers on a chartered plane bound for a Las Vegas gambling trip, instead of the guy she just tried to seduce into having oral sex. *Damn! This is getting weirder by the minute.*

The plane touches down and quickly roars to a stop. Since a private jet is so much smaller than a commercial aircraft, it feels as if we just landed on the deck of an aircraft carrier. Eva walks out of the cockpit as if nothing had happened between us a couple of hours earlier. She unlocks the aircraft door and gestures for me to depart. As I walk past her, she tells me with a big—yet fake—smile on her face, "I hope you enjoyed your flight. Please come again."

"With service like this, how could I not?"

It's the only clever response I can think of. I thought it would sound like something Sean Connery would say in a James Bond film. But when it comes out of my mouth, I just feel like an idiot.

That whole flight was strange. But now I have more pressing matters to attend to. As I pop my head out the jet's door, I immediately hear the sound of waves crashing along the shore of the Mediterranean Sea. Even though it is still dark outside, there is no doubt that we are in Beirut. This is one of my favorite cities in the world. Once known as the "Paris of the Middle East," it is a liberal Arab country, where taboo topics such as alcohol, sex, and Western culture can freely coexist with conservative Muslim traditions, despite years of civil war and confusing political party agendas.

I walk away from the jet toward the private VIP terminal.

I don't bother looking back at Eva. I'm sure we both prefer it that way. Once inside the single-room brick building, a lone, beautiful Lebanese girl in a low-cut blouse greets me from behind a metallic arrivals desk. She has glitter fashionably sprinkled across her ample cleavage, and her eye shadow is painted on like that of Cleopatra. Lebanese women are among the most gorgeous in the world and this young lady is certainly doing nothing to tarnish that reputation. The sheik really knows how to do the whole private travel thing right.

In a flirtatious manner, "Cleopatra" asks if she can summon a car for me. There is no talk of clearing any sort of Immigration or Customs procedures. Apparently, this flight never officially happened.

I tell the girl I need a ride to Le Gray Hotel. She escorts me out front where a white Bentley Flying Spur, with a chauffeur, is ready to whisk me away. Once again, I am impressed by the sheik's style. I check an email on my phone and learn that the initial funds for this consulting engagement have been transferred to my account in Liechtenstein. Life seems surreal right now.

It has been less than seventy-two hours since I received the phone call from the sheik, while being fitted for a suit in Milan. In just that short time I have traveled to Dubai to meet with one of the most powerful men in the Middle East at the Royale Suite in the Burj al-Arab, had $2 million wired to my bank account, flew on a private helicopter, then on a private jet, had turned down getting head from a Bavarian beauty at 30,000 feet, and now I am riding in the back of a Bentley in the middle of the night in Beirut. Yet, instead of feeling proud of my accomplishments, I have a pit in the bottom of my stomach. Something doesn't feel right about this job.

We're driving to the Le Gray, one of the premier hotels in Beirut. Located in the downtown area, it sits along the famous waterfront known as the Corniche and overlooks the historic St. George Beach Club and the recently-built Rafik Hariri Mosque, named in honor the late prime minister who was assassinated by a massive car bomb in 2005.

I've been traveling to Lebanon since the end of the brutal Civil War, which lasted from 1975-1985. I used to stay in the

Phoenician Hotel, another popular five-star accommodation, but once I tried Le Gray, it has been my hotel of choice ever since. It is also intensely discreet, which means you would be hard pressed to ever find a record of me, or any other prior guest.

Its exterior matches the traditional French-inspired façade that is common in the neighborhood, while the interior is a combination of sleek modern architecture and tasteful luxurious furnishings. Another great selling point is that the staff never asks too many questions. Wealthy Gulf Arabs frequently use Le Gray as a rendezvous point to meet their mistresses, while the wives of politicians stay here because it allows them close proximity to Beirut's many high-end shops, such as Cartier, Gucci, and Van Cleef and Arpels.

It's been a long day and I'm looking forward to a good night's sleep.

# THE RUSSIAN

**Location:** *Le Gray Hotel*
**Time:** *0530 hours*

I have awoken early this morning. The familiar moan of the Muslim call to prayer is reverberating outside my window from a nearby mosque. The call to prayer happens five times a day in the Middle East, reminding those of the Islamic faith of their duty to pray to Allah. It is still dark outside, and because I am a light sleeper, I have used this first call as my alarm clock on more than one occasion.

I am anxious to take a walk along the Corniche to get some fresh air and clear my head. So much has happened so quickly that I need to collect my thoughts and formulate a plan for my meeting with Yuri, my Russian contact, later today. The Mediterranean is calm and especially blue as I head out of the lobby. The air is crisp and I can clearly see snowcapped Mount Lebanon off in the distance. One of the more interesting things about Lebanon is that you can actually snow ski in the morning up on the mountaintop and then drive 90 minutes down to the beach and lay out in the sand by lunchtime.

As I walk along the boardwalk, I am surprised to see so many people already out and about. Men are jogging in athletic tracksuits, the ones with the three white stripes down the side. There are numerous fishermen casting long poles, over the rocky coast and out into the sea. Young couples in their teens and early twenties walk hand-in-hand, while at the same time there are women covered from head-to-toe in black *burqas*, shuffling a few steps behind their husbands. Beirut certainly has something for everyone.

This project has me worried. Sheik al-Gaylani has made it sound as though this should be a very simple assignment—just accompany the weapons to the buyer in Afghanistan. I have learned from my past experience that nothing is simple when the country you are traveling to ends in the word "Stan." Plus, I don't trust Russians. I have known too many other consultants who have been burned by their Mafioso way of conducting business. They can be ruthless operators and won't hesitate to cut your throat just to save a few extra dollars, or to eliminate a trail of possible witnesses.

As my walk along the Corniche continues, I see a large vacant lot overgrown with weeds behind a rusted razor wire fence. This is a prime piece of waterfront real estate that is just sitting empty. Then it strikes me what this is—or rather what it was. This used to be the location of the US Embassy that was blown up by terrorists, presumably the group Hezbollah, in the 1980s. It is easy to forget that Beirut was home to some of the bloodiest urban street battles prior to the modern street wars that we later saw, and continue to see, in Bosnia, the Congo, Iraq, Syria, and Libya.

Beirut remains divided by its ironically named "Green Line," a no-man's land right down the middle of the city that once separated warring factions. Today, several pockmarked buildings still stand empty in that zone, painful scars that remind of a time, not too long ago, that saw cousins fighting cousins.

I stop for a strong shot of espresso at a coffee stand, which hangs precariously over the rocky seawall. I immediately feel the caffeine take hold, and my mind finally begins to work. I realize I need to formulate some ground rules for my discussion with Yuri later today. I am an international consultant who is in high demand to some of the world's most notorious political leaders, not a so-called mule who simply accompanies illegal shipments of arms like a DHL driver delivering a package. I will have to make it abundantly clear to Yuri that I have leverage in this deal and I am acting as the sheik's personal representative, not his courier. I am being paid five million dollars for this job for a reason. It will not be a walk in the park, and the sheik—and Yuri—are already keenly aware of this.

I return to my hotel room and call down for some room service. I opt for the traditional Lebanese breakfast of sweet pastries and fruit, accompanied by more coffee and freshly squeezed orange juice. I also request that a local newspaper be provided with the meal. Before the food is delivered, I take a hot shower and then shave. I throw on a comfortable tan, super-150 thread count, wool Brioni suit. I opt for a light-blue button-down oxford shirt from Brooks Brothers and slip on a pair of brown Ferragamo loafers without socks. I want to be comfortable today. By the time my food arrives, I already feel completely refreshed. I instruct the delivery boy that I would like to have my breakfast out on the balcony overlooking the water. He places the serving tray on the outdoor table and I provide him with a handsome tip.

I open the front page of the newspaper and nearly fall out of my chair as I read the headline: AMBASSADOR AND FORMER PRESIDENTIAL CANDIDATE FOUND DEAD IN SEYCHELLES HOTEL ROOM.

My old friend Mr. David has apparently been found hanged by a belt in a luxury resort on the island of Seychelles. According to the article, he was seen entering the hotel the night before with a young woman. He was found by housekeeping with a belt around his neck hanging in his closet. He was completely naked, and it was assumed that he accidentally died of affixation while performing a sexual act. The story continued to report that at least 500 accidental deaths occur each year when individuals choke either themselves, or their partner, while attempting orgasm. This appeared to be the case. The woman who accompanied him the night before was not seen leaving the hotel. An anonymous quote from the ambassador's foreign affairs office read, *"We are all shocked by this recent tragedy, as well as by the immoral behavior that led to the Ambassador's death."*

I have a pretty good idea who the anonymous source was who added that last little insult to injury for Mr. David. It had to have been Mohammed. I am certain Mr. David's death was no accident. I'm also certain it was Mohammed and his brother, the king, simply tying up some loose ends just as precaution. I find myself hoping they don't consider me a loose end, as well. But I can't worry about this now. I have to focus on preparing for my meeting with Yuri.

At exactly one o'clock that afternoon I head up to The Blue Restaurant, conveniently located on the rooftop of the hotel. It is an elegant outdoor setting, which offers some of the finest French cuisine in the country. I was told that Yuri would be easy to spot. He has blond hair, blue eyes, a tall muscular build, and always wears a white suit. It sounded as if I was supposed to meet a Bond villain.

As soon as I walked out to the restaurant, a stunning Lebanese girl, with a low-cut black tank top, greets me at the door. Her surgically enhanced breasts are magnificent and she knows it. She is wearing a white leather skirt, which is just short enough to accentuate her long tanned legs, which look even longer in her four-inch heels. I am instantly smitten with her.

"*Marhaba*," she greets me.

"*Marhaba*," I respond.

"Just one for lunch?" she asks.

"No, I'm meeting someone."

"Too bad," she sighs, pouting like a beautiful woman who knows how to get what she wants from men. "The restaurant is empty and I am looking for someone to chat with. You seem like an interesting man."

"You have no idea," I coolly reply.

"Perhaps later then?"

"What time do you get off work?"

"In a few hours."

"Then why don't you swing by my room on your way out? We can go for a drink by the water. I heard there's an amazing belly-dancing show on the beach."

I'm usually not this forward with women, but I conclude that this girl is full of confidence and I want to match her charisma. More pertinently, I suspect she's a plant—by Yuri, perhaps?

"I'm afraid I'd get in trouble if I did that. We are not supposed to fraternize with guests in the hotel. I would get fired if they saw me go into your room," she blushes.

"Don't worry. I am very discreet."

Suddenly I see the infamous Yuri Berezovsky sitting at a table along the railing, which immediately strengthens my suspicions. Holding a newspaper in his left hand and wearing a bright red tie, which contrasts with his white linen suit, he gestures for me to join him.

I glance at the marvelous Lebanese girl, but the pleasure part of my brain shuts down and I turn my attention to the job at hand. I sit next to Yuri, all business. Our eyes connect as we quickly size each other up. The adjectives that immediately go through my head to describe him are cruel, deceptive, untrustworthy, cunning, and deadly. *Shit, he could be a Bond villain!*

"Hello, Yuri."

"Hello, Noah," he replies. "Pleasure to meet you. Please sit down."

His Russian accent is thick and he smiles at me with yellow, cigarette-stained teeth. His aftershave is tremendously overpowering, as if he used half a bottle on his face. At least it will repel insects while we have our lunch.

"How do you like, Beirut?" he asks.

"I love Beirut. It is one of my favorite cities." I decide to play along with his small talk.

"The women here are beautiful, no?"

"Yes, they are."

"Ha! Then perhaps after our meeting we can go find women out on the beach to take back to our rooms for some fun— nonstop!" It has always amazed me how often Russian English speakers use the word "nonstop" to describe how extreme something can be.

Yuri smiles, pulls out a pack of cigarettes, and offers me one. I wave my hand to refuse.

"So, the sheik wants you to babysit my delivery? I say, fuck the sheik. What do you think about that?"

Keeping calm, I respond. "I think we're both being paid a lot of money to do a job. You do yours and I do mine, and everybody wins. I don't see why that should be an issue."

"It is an issue because the sheik does not trust me, apparently. He thinks I am going to screw him. So he sends you to observe me. But really, what can you do, Mr. Noah? Can you actually prevent me from fucking him over?"

"Do you plan on fucking him over?" I ask.

"No, of course not. It is bad business. Plus, I have, how you say, reputation."

"Good. Then none of us has anything to worry about."

Yuri lights a cigarette from a nondescript pack covered with Arabic writing. He takes in a heavy breath and then blows the smoke out hard through the corner of his mouth. This is immediately followed by a hacking cough that lasts several seconds. Loudly gathering a mouthful of phlegm in his throat, he then spits a yellowish blob over the side of the railing. It is not a very appealing sight before lunch, and I hope nobody is walking along the street below. I have found that Russian table manners essentially don't exist. But I have dealt with Russians before, and many times they act crudely to look tough or to intimidate.

"Ah, sorry. I ate too much pussy last night."

Despite his vulgarity, I notice that Yuri is wearing a Moritz Grossmann Benu wristwatch. The rare German timepiece must have set him back at least $35,000. It certainly isn't something your typical gangster might be educated about. I am starting to believe Yuri might be merely pretending to be a thuggish Russian arms dealer. I recall back to my encounters with Viktor Bout. He would often behave the same way, attempting to conceal his polished, and cultured, business persona, because it might have been perceived as a sign of softness by those less educated.

I decide to call attention to it.

"Yuri, that is an impressive watch you're wearing. What kind is it?"

"I don't know. I took it off a dead man," he said, laughing.

"No, really. Is that a Moritz Grossmann? I have never seen one before."

"It is. You have good taste, Mr. Noah. I see that you are also a fan of watches. I also have a Patek Philippe at home."

I doubt that was a subterfuge. Now I know the type of man I'm dealing with. Yuri is pretending to be a thug in order to appear as though he could kill me just for having a bad day. The whole Russian mob guy thing is just an act. He's basically a consultant just like me, one who casually remarks about $100,000 wristwatches. His business identity is just the character that he has created. He really has no idea what I am capable of, and I'm certain he feels the same about me. This checkmate puts me at ease and we begin to talk specifics of the delivery, ordering a bottle of local Lebanese wine in the process.

Apparently, my job is to fly on a commercial flight to Turkmenistan and link up with Yuri's cargo pilots at a private airport. I will inspect the weapons to ensure that they are all accounted for and from there we will fly into a small airstrip in Jalalabad, Afghanistan. Once we bypass Customs—presumably with a routine bribe to the locals—and unload the weapons into a truck, we will drive them thirty minutes out into the countryside. There we will meet our contact named Ali, who shall repeat to me the secret passphrase provided by Sheik al-Gaylani. The phrase will ensure he is who he says he is, and, more importantly, confirm that Yuri is not simply handing the weapons over to one of his own contacts instead of the real buyer.

Yuri is unaware that a passphrase has been employed. But he has been in this game long enough to know that checks and balances are always incorporated to prevent a delivery from being compromised. If the person receiving the weapons does not respond correctly to my phrase, I will report it to al-Gaylani, who I am certain will unleash holy hell against Yuri.

Yuri and I skip lunch for only a less-than-stellar bottle of wine, which we leave half-full on the table. Neither of us wants to spend any more time with the other than we have to.

"Thank you, Yuri. I look forward to seeing you again next week in Ashgabat."

"As do I, Mr. Noah."

With that, I turn and walk away from the table, leaving Yuri sitting alone with his cigarettes and that shitty bottle of red.

My bad feeling about this deal lingers.

The Lebanese hostess with the amazing rack is back behind the bar when I walk out. She shoots me a look with her deep-brown puppy eyes, but I am too focused on my concerns to give a shit.

To ease my nerves, I go back to my hotel room, take a small bottle of Johnny Walker Black out of the mini-bar, and dump it into a glass. I throw my head back and down the Scotch in one quick shot. *How the hell do I continue to find myself in these situations?* I plunge backward onto the bed and throw my forearm over my eyes. I try to relax but am too tense.

Twenty minutes later there is a soft knock at my door. I pull myself off the bed and quietly move across the room. I peer through the peephole. *What the hell?*

I open the door to the attractive hostess from the restaurant. She is carrying a curved sword in a gold, metallic sheath in her right hand. A pink silk ribbon is tied around the handle, indicating that it is ceremonial item.

"Hi," I say, caught off guard. "What's with the sword? Are you here to hurt me?"

"Maybe I'm here to cut off your dick for treating me like a whore!" she snaps.

Holding up my hands in a sign of surrender, I apologetically reply, "You're right. I am sorry about that. I didn't mean to ignore you. I was trying to focus on my business meeting."

"That's more like it," she smiles. "May I come in?"

"On two conditions," I reply. "First, you tell me your name, and second you tell me why you're carrying that sword."

"My name is Fatima, and the reason I brought this is because I thought you wanted to see a belly-dancing show."

"In that case, come right in."

So the gorgeous woman slips into my room dragging the sword along the carpet beside her.

"Fatima, my name is Noah, and I'm afraid I still don't quite understand why you have a sword with you."

"Well, Noah," she says, pushing me backwards onto to the bed, "let me show you."

She leans the sword against her tanned thighs and proceeds to lift her tank top over her head, exposing a black silk lingerie bra. Without wasting a second, she reaches behind her back and unclasps the garment, which drops to the floor. Her breasts are even more spectacular than I could have imagined. She lifts the sword delicately above her shoulders and balances the curved blade carefully on top of her head. Slowly lowering her arms out to the side, the sword miraculously manages to stay in place. She begins to sway her hips in a rhythmic fashion, the white skirt hanging loosely around her waist rising and falling with each athletic snap of her lower body.

"Perhaps you've never seen this kind of belly-dancing show," she says, smiling.

Lying on my back and leaning up on my elbows, I become mesmerized by the gyrations of Fatima's stomach, hips, and breasts. The dance lasts for roughly thirty seconds before I lean forward and grab one of her wrists. When I pull her forward on top of me the sword falls innocently backward on the floor. We are now face-to-face and, without a word, we begin to kiss passionately. Then a circuit breaker goes off in my head. I am violating one of my cardinal rules. I push Fatima away gently, wondering now if hidden cameras are doing their work.

She grabs the sword and raises it as if to attack.

"Twice you insult me she says. Most men die after one insult."

She storms from my room. I lay on the bed aroused and disturbed. For the next few hours, I forget about Yuri, the sheik, and the incredibly bad deal I just agreed to. Right now, all I can think of is Fatima.

# MR. WINGTIPS

*Location:* *Ashgabat International Airport, Turkmenistan*
*Time:* *0145 hours*

I flew from Beirut back to Europe and then on to Ashgabat, the capital city of Turkmenistan. I was the only person sitting in business class on the small, virtually empty, Lufthansa flight to the former Soviet republic. As a result, I was showered with attention by the two lovely young German flight attendants unfortunate enough to pull this thankless flight route.

The two women, Cecelia and Franziska, were both in their late twenties and adventurous spirits. In fact, at some point during the journey, each took a turn sitting down next to me and sneaking a glass of champagne, while the other one stood watch for anyone who might venture through the curtain up into the business class cabin. We joked about the liberal attitude toward sex in Germany and how it differed from other countries. If I weren't about to walk into a shit storm, I would have arranged to meet up with the two while they were on their layover. But there is a time and a place for everything.

When the plane landed, I wished the girls well and handed them a business card with an untraceable email address and one of my alias names. Maybe, if I get through this consulting engagement without getting chopped into little pieces by Yuri, I will take the girls to dinner on my way back through Frankfurt.

Going through Ashgabat International Airport is like stepping into a time machine; everything is outdated by decades.

Although it is freezing outside with a foot of snow on the ground, there is no heat inside the airport. All of the employees are wearing parkas with fur hats in order to keep warm. Many of them sip hot coffee, which I have no doubt contains a nip of vodka.

I successfully navigate through the immigration counter on a fraudulent Swiss passport, despite receiving harsh questioning from some knuckle-dragging meathead of an officer appropriately named Boris, as identified by his name tag. I stand by the lone baggage carousel, which slowly squeaks around in circles until my $6,500 black Brioni Leather Trolley—the ultimate suitcase crafted from a single piece of leather—tumbles onto the rubber belt from behind a set of dusty plastic flaps. My once-gorgeous bag is now filthy. I'm sure that it has already been examined and pilfered through by the special police before being sent out to me. I don't know if I'm more upset that they opened it or that they scuffed its exterior. Either way, I will buy a new one after this job is done.

Nobody is manning the Customs counter—another clue that my bag has already been searched—so I pass through the sliding doors into the arrivals area. The airport terminal is deserted. Only a janitor is seen sweeping the floors. It now is two in the morning. I walk outside and the parking lot is empty except for a lone taxi driver staying warm in his old Russian Lada. The rusted automobile is smaller than a Mini Cooper and had to have been built in the late 1970s or early '80s. I have no choice but to request his services. Because of the Mongolian influence of Genghis Khan and his horde centuries earlier, many of the locals display Asian features, though it appears that my driver is a mix between Russian and traditional Turkmen—a truly unique look if you are not used to seeing it every day.

As we drive along the dimly lit, unplowed, snow-covered streets, Ashgabat looks like a city frozen in time. One of the last cities to break free of the Soviet influence, its former leader and self-declared President for Life Saparmurat Niyazov—better known as Turkmenbashi—ruled from 1991 until his death in 2006. Typical of a Stalinist dictator, Turkmenbashi, which means "Leader of the Turkmens," had earned the distinction from the diplomatic community as creating the third-largest cult of personality in the world—surpassed only by Saddam Hussein and Kim Jong Il, measured by the number of his images displayed throughout the country.

The highly eccentric ruler had even constructed a life-sized golden statue of himself, arms extending to the sky, which tracked the path of the sun. He also commissioned a massive concrete statue of a bull to be placed in the center of the city, with a solid-gold statue of a baby riding on its shoulders. The baby was said to symbolize Turkmenbashi as an infant, who through divine intervention survived one of the country's worst earthquakes as a toddler, proof that he was "the chosen one" from birth.

Even after Turkmenbashi's death, not much changed in Ashgabat. His successor, President Gurbanguly Berdimuhamedow, only minimally opened up the country to outsiders, and it still ranks as having one of the worst human rights records on Earth.

A landlocked country wedged between Iran, Afghanistan, Kazakhstan, Uzbekistan, and Turkmenistan, sits in a tough geographical neighborhood. The terrain is a combination of jagged mountains and a harsh, black-sand desert. The weather has two seasons: extremely hot and miserable and extremely cold and miserable. The architecture is still that of the drab communist influence, and small, boxy Ladas still drive up and down the poorly maintained streets. Only now the nouveau-riche Russian mafia types rule this desolate nation, which has become a hub for gray arms dealers, narcotraffickers, and modern day slave traders. It is truly one of the last great, untamed regions of the world—a land that time forgot, much like the American Wild West of the mid-1800s.

For a guy like me, though, it's that Frank Sinatra line, "My kind of town."

I booked a room at a lesser-known hotel in order to stay under the government's radar. The nicer hotels are owned by the local intelligence service. As a result, all of the rooms are wired with audio and video surveillance that keep tabs on foreign visitors. I check in to a four-story concrete cube of a hotel and pay with US dollars—the preferred currency in this part of the world. The old man behind the desk, who reminds me of Doctor Zhivago, smiles when I hand him the wad of cash.

A bellboy, who insists on carrying my Brioni trolley, accompanies me to my room on the top floor. There is no elevator, and we walk up the four flights in an unlit stairwell that reeks of urine. I can hear the sounds of people moaning from sex as we ascend the stairs. There are probably plenty of prostitutes on duty in this shady establishment tonight.

The bellboy inserts a large brass key, which looks better suited for a lock from medieval times, into the room door. My temporary dwelling can only be described as Spartan at best. There is one twin bed, one dresser, and one chair. No desk or TV. A radiator under the window provides the only semblance of heat. The view is of the dank streets below. The bathroom is not much better. The cracked white tiles are stained with rust and water spots, and the once-transparent shower curtain is now nearly opaque from black mold. At least nobody would expect to find me here. Then again, it would also be the perfect place for someone to leave me for dead. The things a whore consultant like me will do for $2 million.

I decide to take a shower and try to relax. But there is only cold, dirty water flowing through the pipes. I shiver as the brownish liquid washes over me. I lather up using my Tom Ford body wash, as opposed to the tiny, unwrapped bar of soap, which has been conveniently provided for me in the tub and has a dark hair prominently displayed on it—evidence that I am not its first customer. For sanitary reasons, I use my own towel to dry off. Over the past ten years I have made it a habit to always pack my lucky "Gatorade" towel—the one with multiple Gatorade logos, just like the one seen on television and used on the sidelines at various sporting events by athletes such as Michael Jordan, Lionel Messi, and Peyton Manning. Whether I'm in a jungle, a war zone, or a seven-star hotel, my Gatorade towel is always at the ready. It is one of the last remaining items of my past life—a life I do not speak of anymore.

I change into a pair of running shorts and T-shirt and settle onto the lumpy bed. I'm sure these same sheets have been frequently stained with bodily fluids over the years, but I try not to think about it. I pull a large bottle of Evian water from my travel bag, along with a bar of Toblerone chocolates I had picked up at the duty free shop. This will be my dinner tonight. I also retrieve the copy of the latest book I'm reading, *Leadership*, by legendary UCLA college basketball coach, John Wooden. I like to study the mindset of winners, regardless of their chosen field. My efforts have included the philosophies of generals, politicians, religious leaders, businessmen, and sports coaches. I am always hungry to understand what guiding principles helped them to achieve success. Unfortunately, I am doubtful Coach Wooden ever had to deal with corrupt Arab sheiks or Russian mobsters during his career. Within an hour, I am asleep with the book on my chest and all of the lights on in the room.

I awake to a knock at my door. My heart is racing and for a moment I don't know where I am. This is actually quite common for me, considering my frequent crisscrossing of time zones. I spring out of bed and quietly move across the room toward the door. Whoever is on the other side, I don't want them to know I am in the room. I carefully put my eye to the peephole and am surprised to see two female figures standing within the concave image. Is that Cecilia and Franziska, the two flight attendants with whom I was flirting just a few hours earlier? *How in the world did they find me?*

I cautiously open the door and discover that instead of the two German girls, I am actually standing face-to-face with two Russian prostitutes replete in high heels and low-cut evening dresses—one in a bright-red sequined gown and the other in a piece made of thin white silk and virtually see-through. The cleavage on each of these two blonde bombshells is so astounding I have trouble looking either of them in the eyes. They are both tall and very pretty, but I can't make out their ages.

My mind is still in a fog. *Why are they here? Why are they dressed like they are about to attend a black-tie gala in Moscow?*

"Good evening, darling," says one of the women in a thick accent. "We thought you might like some company."

"I'm sorry, but I think that you have the wrong room." I attempt to close the door, but the woman quickly presses her hand against it, preventing it from shutting.

"You don't understand. We saw you check in, and we want to party with you."

"I'm busy," I rudely reply.

"Come on, darling, don't you want to play with us? I have cocaine and we are both so horny."

"I want to do line of coke off your dick," the other girl chimes in with a sultry accent.

"Sorry," I repeat, as I abruptly close the door in their faces.

This was certainly not a coincidence. Yuri knows where I'm staying. I must be under surveillance by him and his men right now. He must have contacts at the airport, or the old man at the desk was obligated to report any guests to the local intelligence service—a service which no doubt is on the take to a wealthy man like Yuri.

*Shit!* I have seen this movie before. I ran the same scam in Africa on Mr. David. Only this time I am the mark, and Yuri is playing out my role. I try to go back to bed, but my mind is racing. I stare at the alarm clock until it reaches 6 a.m. and decide to head down to breakfast.

I descend the four flights of stairs to the lobby. Because of near-freezing temperatures, I am wearing a gray wool turtleneck sweater, a pair of Levi's jeans, wool athletic socks, and black leather Armani boots. I'm still cold but my mind is preoccupied with other things—namely, why Yuri had tried to set me up last night.

The lobby is empty and quiet. I am not surprised to see no one manning the reception desk. Doctor Zhivago must still be asleep. There is, however, a fire burning strongly in the fireplace. I am suddenly startled to see a man in an overcoat and dark suit sitting in a chair next to the fire. He looks like he's been there for hours. He's reading the newspaper and our eyes meet as if he was expecting me. He appears to be a guest at the hotel, but I am also wondering if he was the one who built the fire. I can tell he is sizing me up.

After two very long seconds, his eyes revert back to his paper. He is in his mid-to late fifties—and has a black mustache peppered with gray hairs. He looks very serious and possibly important. His body language is clearing communicating, "Fuck off."

I take a mental photograph of this character and make a particular effort to get a good look at his shoes. It's an old trick I learned from a buddy of mine who used to work with the KGB. He told me that he would pay attention to people's shoes whenever he thought he was under surveillance. The idea is that surveillance team members may change their clothing or put on a disguise, but they rarely change out their shoes during an operation. This guy is wearing polished black wingtips with laces. Not exactly the most comfortable option for conducting foot surveillance. Maybe I'm getting paranoid in my old age.

I make my way to the empty dining area, where a short, heavyset old woman—also with a mustache—greets me with a toothless smile and deeply creased face. Perhaps she is the old man's wife. She gestures me to sit anywhere I want. Perhaps Mr. Wingtips and I are the only guests right now.

There is no buffet set up in the dining area. The old woman approaches my table with a cup of coffee and a piece of bread with a packet of butter on the side. This must be the continental breakfast. No matter, I'm not really hungry, anyway. I slug down the coffee in less than a minute then signal the woman for a refill by holding up the empty mug. As I do this, I notice Mr. Wingtips entering the dining area. He takes a seat at the opposite corner of the room with his back to the wall. He wants to see everything. He opens his ever-present newspaper and his face disappears behind the headlines. I suspect he might be assigned to keep tabs on me. This wouldn't be the first time that I had a minder in a foreign country.

After my second cup of coffee, I decide I will test Mr. Wingtips. I quickly run up to my room and grab my coat. I return to the lobby only to see Mr. Wingtips sitting back in his chair by the fireplace. He must be waiting for me. I quickly make my way out the front of the hotel and take a right down the desolate street. When I come to the first corner, I turn as if I am going to make a left across the intersection. With my shoulders now perpendicular to the front of the hotel, I can easily see Mr. Wingtips walk out the front door while speaking into his cell phone. My suspicions have been confirmed. I am not alone in Ashgabat at the moment.

I walk one more block before I see a street sweeper in a lime-green jumpsuit reach into his pocket and pull out a cell phone. In this country, street sweepers only make a few dollars per day, so it's doubtful he could afford a cell phone. I must be walking through the middle of what's known as a surveillance zone. In this technique, essentially, each city block is covered visually by an operative conducting static surveillance in a fixed location. The target—in this case, me—walks through the zone and the team observes my movements. I'm positive that Mr. Wingtips is back in my room rummaging through my Brioni bag.

*Screw that asshole!* I make my first available left turn and then start heading back toward the hotel. If I walk briskly enough, I might catch him in the act before his men can signal my return. Within sixty seconds I am back in the lobby. I pick up the pace and take the stairs two at a time until I reach my room with my key at the ready. I unlock the door and see that my suitcase has been turned over on my bed.

"Dammit!" I say out loud.

The bastard got in and out before I could catch him.

Nothing is missing. I didn't bring a laptop on this trip, and my cell phone is in my pocket. There were no electronics for him to exploit.

The phone in my room, a heavy old model like something in an Alfred Hitchcock movie, suddenly rings loudly.

"Hello?" I say with a hint of irritability in my voice.

"Ah, Noah, my good friend, you made it!" says a cheery Yuri on the other end of the phone.

"How did you know I was here, Yuri?" I ask with clear anger in my tone.

"Oh, Mr. Noah, I know everything that goes in Ashgabat. It is a small town and people talk."

"Apparently so. How about the guy who was just in my room? What did he tell you?"

"A man in your room? I know nothing about this. I sent you the girls last night but apparently you rejected them. Do you prefer men? I'll note it for next time," he laughs.

I'm no longer able to contain myself. "Listen, motherfucker, I'm done playing games! I know what you're up to. Now, we're going to quickly conclude our business and then go our separate ways. Do you understand?"

"Be careful what you say, Mr. Noah. You are not in Europe anymore. Many people have gone missing in this part of the world for lesser comments. I am your only friend right now. Play by my rules or you might not make it back to the airport."

Unfortunately, Yuri is 100 percent correct. He knows he's got me over a barrel. Even if I tried to make a run for it to the airport right now, his henchmen would probably intercept me and drive me straight out to the desert, where I would be buried alive and have the vultures peck out my eyes. I am indeed forced to play by his rules.

"You win, Yuri. Tell me where to meet you," I say, without trying to sound deflated.

"Good, Mr. Noah. I am glad you see it my way. I will send a car to pick you up in thirty minutes. It will take you to my location where the plane is waiting to fly us to Afghanistan."

With that, the phone line goes dead. I am starting to wonder how much time I have left in this life.

# THE DESERT

*Location:* *Karakum Desert, Turkmenistan*
*Time:* *1400 hours*

I am riding in the back of an old and nondescript van, looking out the dusty windows at the vast, blackish sand of the Karakum Desert, which covers 70 percent of the country. Karakum translates literally to "black sand" in Turkic. It gives me an idea of what the astronauts, who drove their buggy across the surface of the moon, must have felt like.

Three hours ago, I had paid my bill in cash to the old man at the front desk—the same man who probably informed Yuri of my whereabouts—and waited out front of the hotel for my ride. As Yuri promised, a vehicle arrived promptly to take me to wherever I'm supposed to be going. The driver and the other man sitting in the passenger seat look more like fishermen than the Russian henchmen I normally would have expected. They don't speak English, so the three of us sit quietly during the drive.

This is one of the most desolate places on the planet. The desert, which stretches for miles all around me, is so bleak and uninhabitable that I almost expect to see a band of post-apocalyptic bikers appear, straight out of a *Mad Max* movie. I know that if the two thugs sitting in front of me want to kill me, all they need do is push me out of the vehicle and let the desert swallow me alive.

While I continue to entertain that cheery thought, the van begins to slow. I get a queasy feeling. We pull to the side of the empty, two-lane road. No words are exchanged; we just wait for something to happen. Then I begin to hear a faint buzzing noise in the distance. It grows louder. The man in the passenger seat gets out of the van and walks onto the pavement. I watch him and then the plane, which is descending out of a yellowish sky.

I decide to get out of the van as well. My handlers pay me no mind—for one thing, where could I go? I watch the plane, still about a kilometer away. It appears to be a dual-propeller aircraft, perhaps a DC-3, which means it could be over sixty years old. Loud and clunky, the Douglas Cargo models have been reliable workhorses over the decades. The aircraft lines up for its final approach. It's going to land on the road. Its engines roar as the pilot reverses propeller pitch and begins braking.

As the plane draws closer, its backdraft kicks up sand everywhere. I shield my eyes with my forearm, while the man standing beside me feels the urge to take the blast head on. He sticks out his chest and holds his head high as the plane taxis to a stop a few meters in front of him. He smiles as if this were the best part of his day.

The aircraft's propellers eventually rotate to a stop. This bird is even older than I thought. It looks like a rusted tin can and reminds me of the planes in all those Indiana Jones movies.

A side door folds inward, and an attendant lowers a small set of stairs to the ground. Then Yuri pops his head out through the opening. *How convenient. The man himself has chosen to grace us with his presence.* He is wearing a pair of aviator sunglasses and a leather bomber jacket, as if he were the pilot rather than just the owner. The actual pilot, an older Russian man, looks so worn out he could have just woken up after an all-night bender. He follows Yuri, who descends the steps and walks across the dusty road toward me.

"Ah, Mr. Noah, you made it!" He's grinning like a Cheshire cat.

"Wouldn't have missed it for the world," I respond dryly.

"Shall we head for Afghanistan? I know you are probably eager to babysit this delivery so you can report back to the sheik."

"You worry about your job, and I'll worry about mine." I try to sound as though I still have some leverage in my current situation.

"Very well then." With that, Yuri turns to his side and extends his arm, as if to say, "after you."

We proceed up the steps and back into the plane. The interior looks even more beat up than the exterior. There are no seats, just wooden benches with some cargo nets along both sides. Dozens of crates of varying sizes are strapped down near the tail—obviously the weapons we'll be delivering to the Taliban, or some other ragtag group of tribal fighters. They're a combination of AK-47s, land mines, rocket-propelled grenades (RPGs) with launchers, and thousands of rounds of ammunition. The crates are why I am here. They, this relic of an aircraft, and these Russian thugs are how I am going to earn my commission.

I settle into a spot on one of the benches and strap myself in a seatbelt. I doubt it would be of much help should we go down. We're basically sitting among large amounts of explosive material. If we crashed, we'd no doubt go up in a huge ball of flame anyway.

Yuri sits across from me and lights a cigarette.

"Is that really a good idea around all these materials?" I ask.

"You worry too much," he says dismissively.

At that moment, the pilot reenters through the exterior door. I hope he was out inspecting the plane for damage after the landing. More likely, he was pissing. In his right hand he carries a bottle of Stolichnaya vodka and in his left is a roll of silver duct tape. I can't decide which item is more disturbing. Our ride is a sixty-year-old piece of flying scrap metal, held together with duct tape, and guided by a pilot who is probably an alcoholic. We are about to fly over the Hindukush Mountains, which harbor some of the harshest wind conditions on Earth, while sitting on a ton of ammunition and explosives. I look at Yuri, the Russian arms dealer, sitting across from me enjoying his nicotine, and I have to laugh. If I get through this, it will make one helluva story.

The engines roar and the propellers begin to spin. The plane jerks forward as the pilot releases the parking brake. After a surprisingly long takeoff run down the desert road, the plane's wheels leave the ground. As it ascends bumpily into the sky, I see the van with its two occupants slowly disappear below us. Taking in the vastness of the Karakum at this altitude, I realize I had been traveling at the end of the Earth.

The plane banks hard as we change direction. Next stop, the Federally Administered Tribal Area between Afghanistan and Pakistan. Better known as the FATA—one of the last no-man's lands left on the planet—I calculate my odds of surviving this caper as one chance in four.

# WARLORDS
## III

# THE FATA

*Location:* Somewhere over the Federal Administered Tribal Areas of
Afghanistan (FATA)
*Time:* 1700 hours

As the old cargo aircraft sputters through the thin air above
the Hindukush, the view below is mesmerizing. The terrain
is an endless series of jagged rock formations, with some
peaks exceeding four miles in elevation, and each gorge and
crevasse appears more ominous than the next. For centuries,
this precarious land has stubbornly resisted the advances of
civilization. Many proud peoples have tried to annex and remold
the country known as the place where empires go to die, which
is evident by the war-torn and scarred mountainside. Genghis
Khan, Alexander the Great, the British Empire, the Soviets, and
the United States all invaded Afghanistan, only to eventually
retreat either in defeat or frustration. Afghanistan remains a
black hole, refusing to be forced into joining modern civilization.

If Afghanistan is an untamable country, then the FATA is
the equivalent to its roughest neighborhood, into which the
police, military, or anyone with common sense would never
want to venture. This place is like the land that time forgot. It
is inhabited by thousands of illiterate, tribal people living in the
same conservative Islamic fashion as the Prophet Mohammad
did nearly a millennium and a half ago.

The formal boundaries of Afghanistan itself, as is the case
with so many nations, resulted from political decisions by the

major powers of the day. In the mid-19th century, an agreement between the British Empire and Russia established the northern border. And in the late 1800s, the Durand Line marked the southern border and a treaty between British India and Afghan Amir. Uninvited to the negotiations, were many leaders of the Pashtun tribes inhabiting the border areas, and the FATA encompassed tribal villages that sat directly on either side of the invisible lines. As time progressed, it turned out that no one could enforce jurisdiction in this remote region. It became its own lawless country within a failed state. More recently, the FATA has become a radical Islamist haven where Western ideology is not tolerated, and only groups such as al-Qaeda and the Taliban are allowed passage.

Weapons are the ultimate currency in this post-apocalyptic wasteland. Guns equal power despite the ironic fact that these weapons are products of the modern world. That is where I—and Yuri and the sheik—come in. Again, I am strictly an observer assigned to verify the transaction that is soon to unfold on the ground below, much like an impartial, third-party lawyer.

* * *

We have been flying for hours and I feel the plane begin to descend. It cannot happen soon enough. My ears are buzzing and my head is throbbing from the smell of airplane fuel. There is a queasy sensation in the pit of my stomach. I have a very bad feeling about what awaits me.

Because of the vast mountain walls, which surround us on all sides like an enormous salad bowl, a straight-on approach for the plane to land is impossible. Therefore, the DC-3 is forced to spiral down in a corkscrew fashion. I scan the dusty orange-colored ground below and am not surprised to learn that a landing strip is nonexistent. This is going to be a hard landing along packed dirt. The plane tilts to one side and we begin to circle down. I feel the gravitational force getting stronger as we descend as if we had been flushed down a toilet. Now I know a little bit what fighter pilots must feel.

The plane slams down violently and my spine compresses like an accordion. I am thrust forward on my bench and the red straps of the seatbelt dig into my waist and shoulder blades. I look at Yuri sitting across from me and see that the landing has barely caused him to drop any ash from his still-lit cigarette. He must have made this type of landing dozens of times. Maybe this should be reassuring to me. Nevertheless, I begin to have a strange feeling about what lays directly on the other side of that thin oval door.

I hear the propellers slow but the dust that has been stirred up makes it impossible to see anything out my tiny window. The reflection of the hot sun off the metallic wings of the plane casts an explosion of white light, forcing me to squint my eyes. Suddenly, the dust begins to settle and I can see something other than rocks for the first time. It is a human figure. No, it is several human figures—dozens of them. I also see pack mules. I see guns. Lots and lots of guns. Russian-made Kalashnikovs to be precise, or AK-47s as they are more commonly known.

"We're here, Comrade Yuri!" I hear the pilot yell back in our direction.

Yuri takes the cigarette from between his lips and drops it on the floor of the plane. Crushing it with his boot, he looks at me with his devilish smirk and says, "Are you ready to go to work, Mr. Noah?"

"Always," I reply with a look of confidence. Only on the inside, my heart must be racing at 150 beats per minute.

The pilot opens the squeaky door of the plane and drops the staircase to the rocky ground with a thud. He then steps back inside the cockpit, allowing Yuri and I to deplane first. Yuri exits and disappears quickly into the hot sun. I hesitate in the doorway.

Standing before us, encircling the airplane, must be fifty Taliban king warriors. They are all wearing dust-stained white man pajamas (essentially baggy pants with a long hanging shirt). They all have tiny knit caps and worn sandals. I cannot imagine how they traverse the mountains wearing those things, but they obviously do. Most of them are wearing what look like military vests, carrying a vast array of additional ammunition magazines for their rifles, along with a few dangling Russian-made hand grenades. Others have imposing knives tucked into their belts—I fear they might be used for beheadings. All of the men have long dark beards, which are frightfully imposing. Even more imposing are the rumors of the Taliban's brutal rapes against men and women—even sheep!

Yuri shakes hands with one of the larger members of the group. He must be the leader. His beard is also noticeably dyed a reddish color with henna. This must signify his position as the warlord. Yuri speaks with him in what sounds like a perfect *Pashtun*, the native dialect of the FATA. The two men look very serious in their discussion. Suddenly, Yuri turns and points at me, still standing in the doorway. Both Yuri and the warlord break into big smiles. In an instant, I am jolted forward. The pilot has come up behind me and pushed me out the door. I land face first on the rocky ground below. My hands tear across shard stones and my palms begin to bleed. Yuri begins to laugh heartedly.

"What the fuck was that?" I demand to Yuri.

"That was me delivering you to the Taliban, along with all these weapons," he replies.

"What?"

"You foolish, foolish man, Noah! Did you actually think that you were going to fly all the way to the FATA just to witness a business transaction with a warlord?"

"Yuri, why are you doing this? We are both professionals who are just doing our jobs. I mean you no harm. Just give these guys their weapons and let's get out of here."

"Oh, Noah. You still don't get it, do you? Yuri begins. "You see, I have been following behind you, around the globe, for years. I have lost repeated consulting jobs because of you. Always coming in second for a multimillion-dollar project. Our clients are the same—kings, sheiks, warlords, and dictators. Unfortunately, these nefarious clients are becoming scarcer as the world becomes smaller, thanks to the internet and 24-7 media reporting. There is no room for men like us to compete anymore. Therefore, it is time for you to officially retire and allow me my turn as the number one adviser to the world's worst leaders.

"This is insane!" is all I can muster.

"Oh shut up, already. With every word you say the more upset I become for losing any projects to a weaker man like you in the first place."

I finally get to my feet and try to regain my composure.

"Listen to me, Yuri. I never claimed to be the best in the business. In fact, you and I are in totally different lines of business, with different clients."

"Don't talk to me as if I am an idiot! Or I swear that I will gut you right here and leave you for the vultures to pick at your sun-cooked corpse!"

"Yuri, listen to me please. If we join forces, we can become the most powerful consultants in history. We will double our profits and it will allow us to enter into all new markets. Not only that, you have my word that once we have built our empire, I will bow out and turn it all over to you."

"And why would you do that?"

"Because my goal was to retire to the Caribbean and spend the rest of my days fishing, drinking rum, and fucking exotic island women. I don't give a shit about being a consultant anymore. I've made tens of millions; I don't need more money . . . So, what do you say? Let's join forces. Hell, I will even give you all of my existing clients right now, with glowing referrals!"

I stand quietly in anticipation, waiting for Yuri's reply. The warlord studies me then looks at Yuri. I don't think he understands what is going on. For this, he is losing patience. If there isn't resolution soon between Yuri and I, violence could ensue. A mule gives out a loud hawing sound, and some of the Taliban fighters can be heard questioning each other in Pashtun.

"Noah, your bullshit doesn't work with me as it did with those bumbling idiots in Africa," Yuri finally retorts. "Oh, you didn't know that you stole the job of slandering Jing Ping from me? I wanted that project for months and I lost out to your pathetic ass. You apparently convinced Mohammed that you were the best man for the job. For that reason alone I am going to leave you in the good hands of my friend here, Whalid bin Talibani—a warlord regarded as the nastiest sonofabitch in the entire FATA."

The old warlord hears his name being mentioned and puffs his chest out with pride. His men also let out a chant of "Whalid!" in unison.

I realize it now. I'm fucked.

Talibani approaches me and stands inches from my face. I can smell his breath, which apparently has never experienced a toothbrush or mouthwash. It smells like a cat shit in his mouth and then proceeded to follow it in there to die. I try to keep my composure. Talibani stands over six feet tall and is built like a steel worker. Although his face is tanned and covered with deep creases, putting his age at around sixty, his physique has been chiseled from a lifetime of hiking through these treacherous Afghan mountains and killing countless enemies on the battlefield. I can see bloodstains on the large curved knife tucked into his belt.

The intimidating Talibani looks me up and down and decides I would be an easy person to kill. I am hoping that he just kills me quickly with a bullet between the eyes. The horrific alternative would most assuredly include me being ass-raped by this filthy behemoth, along with a group of his men. Raping a male combatant in the FATA is done to humiliate and injure their enemies. Right now I must look like fresh meat in my Western blue jeans and turtleneck.

At that moment, I hear the steady buzz of the ramp of the airplane being lowered. The pilot is ready to unload the weapons for the mountain fighters.

"Well, Noah, your last job as a consultant was to observe delivery of these weapons for the sheik. Perhaps you should get to work." Yuri laughs.

"And what about the sheik? Was he in on this deal?"

"Of course, he was! I told him that I would give him a thirty-percent discount if he made up that story about you needing to observe delivery of weapons. In fact, I even fronted the down payment he gave you. I hope you spent that money already because I am afraid that you won't have another opportunity."

"Yuri, I had no idea that I made you feel so insecure. Perhaps, you had issues with your mother when you were a child. Or maybe you just have a small dick." I say it sarcastically, trying not to allow him the satisfaction of knowing that I'm scared shitless.

Yuri smirks at me.

Then I think of one more lie as a last-ditch effort to keep him from leaving me with the warlord and his men.

"Yuri, you should know that a man like me always has a contingency plan. Should I not return home, a hit squad will be activated to hunt you down and torture you. An enormous sum of money will be automatically wired to them when I don't return and another sum will be wired when you are killed."

"You're full of shit until your last breath, Noah," says Yuri. "Even if you are telling the truth, I'll take my chances."

"You really want to take that risk? Cut me loose, and you have my word that you'll never see me again. Otherwise, you will spend the remainder of your short life looking over your shoulder for a hit team to snatch you off the street or from your bed."

"You must be a remarkable poker player, Noah." Yuri laughs. "Even when you clearly hold no cards, you still like to bluff. You were a worthy adversary until the end. But, I have finally proven to you, and the rest of the people in our tiny consulting universe, that I am the best. Goodbye, Noah."

Talibani is still standing inches from my face with a stare that could kill. He opens his mouth into a smile to reveal his few remaining brown teeth. His hot breath smells even worse.

I give a slight smile back.

The last thing I recall is Talibani leaning his head backwards before furiously slamming his solid forehead into mine.

For a split second I see a white flash of light. Then everything goes dark.

# DIRTY TOENAILS

**Location:** *Somewhere within the FATA, along the Afghanistan-Pakistan border*
**Time:** *Unknown*

So here I am, prepared to die. I am on my knees before a machete-wielding warlord in what I can only assume is a hut somewhere in the FATA. I am bound and dressed in an orange jumpsuit with piss running down my leg. Yuri and the sheik have sold me out to eliminate business competition. My remaining moments on Earth are now at the sanction of the merciless Whalid Talibani. My soul is filled with loneliness, regret, and, yes—terror—even for a guy like me who has thrived in life and death situations.

I see the warlord's equally imposing tribesmen eyeing me from either side of his massive frame with fiendish grins. I think of a horror worse than death—being raped by these filthy savages.

I try to hold it together, but eventually I hang my head and cry. Not for fear of death, but rather the disappointment of living such a selfish and unfulfilled existence. I certainly had talents, but I used them for only the most worthless of purposes. I could have done so much better with my life. What happened to that nice kid that I used to be just thirty years ago? Where did my normal life get off track?

Then something snaps inside, and my fear turns to anger. *Fuck these assholes!* If I can somehow get them to cut me loose,

I will kill each one of them with my bare hands. I have enough left in me to break each of their necks.

"Cut me loose and kill me like a man!" I shout at the warlord. "You call yourself a fighter? Cut me loose and fight me!"

The men are surprised by my sudden outburst. It is apparent that they do not understand English but do, in fact, comprehend my demand. Talibani just laughs. The butt of the rifle slams into the back of my head. The warlord raises his knife and screams at me in his native *Pashtun,* while the other two take turns kicking my sides.

"Cut me loose and fight me like a man!" I repeatedly scream, while being flogged and beaten.

It is no use. My adrenaline rush is fading and I am starting to lose my small burst of strength. The kicks continue and a squarely placed kick across the jaw finally silences me. I'm on my side and can only see one of the men's sharp and dirty toenails in their worn-out sandals in front of my nose. In one last determined effort, I crawl up on my knees with my hands still behind my back. I look up at the warlord directly in his eyes.

"Just shoot me, for God's sake," I mumble. "Put a bullet between my eyes. Get it over with!"

For the first time in my life I am completely unafraid and fully prepared to die.

I hang my head and close my eyes. I whisper one last prayer asking for forgiveness and begging for a quick bullet rather than a slow knife.

I hear the crack of a rifle being fired. My prayer was apparently answered. But I feel no pain. *Has death come so quickly I didn't even feel it?* Then I hear two more shots. Could they have missed me the first time? What the hell is happening?

I open my eyes and lift my head. The three men are all crumpled on the ground in front of me. It appears that the two masked men, who were just seconds before disguising their faces, have had their skulls blown open. Whalid Talibani, the feared warlord, is motionless on his back, staring upwards into eternity. Bright red blood clashes against the color of white brain matter and bone fragments, as it leaks onto the dirty ground and pools into a brownish puddle around my knees. *Am I dreaming?* More gunshots erupt and my vision is obstructed by white smoke. My eardrums ring from the deafening crack of gunfire.

Suddenly, a voice calls out to me. "Sir, are you alright?"

I look up to see a large man dressed in all black staring down at me. He is wearing a helmet and night-vision goggles. His shirtsleeves are pulled up to his elbows, and I see a tattoo of Abraham Lincoln on one of his massive forearms. He has brought others with him. There must be ten of these men.

"Sir, can you walk? We need to move. Right now!"

Before I can answer, two of the others pick me up by my arms and lift me to my feet. They cut off the ropes binding my hands and legs. I have an arm over each man's shoulders and we are quickly scurrying out a door, leaving the corpses of six men and one goat. There is a line of eight massive armored trucks waiting outside in the cold night air. They are all painted black. Half are pickups with large-caliber machine guns mounted on their beds, each manned by one of these mysterious soldiers. It reminds me again of something from a *Mad Max* film.

I pause for a second to look up at the bright starry sky. The full moon as it sits above the snowcapped mountains around us. I can see my breath in the moonlight. I think, *This place is beautiful. Life is beautiful.*

One of the men carrying me barks in my ear, "Hey asshole, wake up! We're not out of this yet!"

I quickly rejoin reality and nod in agreement.

My escorts throw me into the back of what I can only assume is an armored SUV and box me in, one sitting on each side. The line of vehicles begins to move rapidly as we traverse the incredibly bumpy mountain roads. I feel myself leaning forward, so we must obviously be moving downhill. "Abraham Lincoln" is, I think, the team leader. He asks me questions while the other man—probably a medic—inspects me for bullet holes and other injuries.

"What's your name?" asks Lincoln.

"It doesn't matter," I automatically reply as I've done thousands of times before.

"Pull your head out of your ass and tell me your goddamn name or I'll throw you out onto the road!" Now I'm certain he's the team leader.

For the first time in almost ten years I tell someone—a stranger—my real name.

"It's Paul."

It feels good to tell the truth.

"Okay, Paul. What else can you tell me about yourself?"

Maybe it's finally time to come clean about my past. Mr. Lincoln, still wearing his black helmet and sporting a thick scraggly beard, is in for an interesting tale. I hold nothing back.

"I was born in Detroit to Scottish immigrants. I turned forty-five last week. I got my law degree from the University of Michigan. I have an ex-wife and two children I haven't seen or heard from in over a decade. Many years ago I was well on my way to becoming a successful lawyer, specializing in international trade negotiations. While at a symposium in Geneva, I met a man who claimed to be a headhunter for a strategic management firm. He asked me if I might be interested in a part-time job as an international consultant . . . " I blather on, the words slurring from my swollen face.

# ICE MAN

*Location:* Undisclosed military base, Afghanistan
*Time:* Unknown

I tell Abraham and his other three colleagues in the armored SUV pretty much everything I could think of about my various adventures across the globe. At one point the medic jokingly asks if my company is currently hiring. He says he's never flown first class before. I tell him that after this experience I suspect there will be a consulting position opening up in the near future.

Considering what I have just gone through, I feel completely at ease with my rescuers, though I still don't know who exactly they are. They certainly sound American and I clearly notice an American velcro flag patch on to the left shoulder of the guy in the passenger seat. Eventually the driver turns on some music. Lynyrd Skynyrd's Southern-fried rock 'n roll ballad, "Simple Man," blares from the speakers. Now I'm certain they're from the United States.

"Hey, you guys SEALs?"

"Not exactly," says Lincoln.

At that moment we pull up to a steel gate with massive concrete walls, dirt barriers, sand bags, and razor wire all around. It looks like a fortress that it meant to keep out zombies. The gate slides open ever so slightly and another one of these ninja warriors, dressed completely in black and armed to the teeth, steps out from behind. He blinds us through the windshield with a large flashlight. He wants to be sure that the bad guys are not coming through the gate Trojan horse style. Once our identities are confirmed, we pass through the barrier only to be stopped by another gate. We are now boxed in on both the front and the back of the SUV. A four-man team begins to examine the exterior and underneath our truck. I can only assume that they are looking for magnetic IEDs that have been affixed to the armor. I suddenly realize that I have no idea where the other vehicles in our convoy have gone.

We clear our final safety inspection and I am driven into a courtyard.

"We're here," says a relaxed team leader Lincoln.

"Holy shit, I didn't thank you guys!" I suddenly blurt out, realizing I'm a bigger idiot than before.

"Don't mention it. It's what we do."

"No, seriously. You guys risked your life to save a worthless piece of shit like me! Thank you!"

"When you put it that way, we should have just stayed home and played Halo on the Xbox," Mr. Lincoln sheepishly replies.

At that moment, an older gentleman approaches in the darkness. I can hear the crunch of gravel under his boots as he moves nearer. He is tall and burly, at least my height, but probably weighs close to 275 pounds. He has a bright white beard, is dressed in cargo pants and a short-sleeved, buttoned down fishing shirt, and is wearing a baseball cap from The George Washington University. *What's with all the presidential references?* At least it confirms I'm on a US base of some sort.

He extends his hand and speaks. "Sir, welcome back to Afghanistan. My name is Ice Man."

Ice Man? Seriously? This guy's a fan of *Top Gun*?

"Thank you," I mutter.

"Why don't we get you into our medical room so the doc can check you out. Then we'll get you a hot shower and a home-cooked meal. Sound good?"

"Sure!" is all I can think to respond.

After a thorough medical exam and two bags of intravenous saline solution to rehydrate me, I am allowed to take a hot shower. Water has never felt so good against my skin. I have grit and sand uncomfortably stuck in all my crevasses. I reek of body odor. An Afghan goat probably smells better right now.

To make matters worse, I feel humiliated as I wash off the dried urine between my legs. I can't believe I pissed myself.

I turn off the water in the shower, which is in some sort of makeshift locker room facility. Ice Man is standing outside the curtain when I step through in a towel. He offers me a set of his clothes, a GWU sweatshirt and sweatpants, plus an oversized pair of Crocs. So much for my designer Tom Ford suit and Ferragamo shoes.

"Now, let's get you some chow."

"Sure," I say again.

We walk twenty meters across the compound to another trailer. This one is slightly bigger than the others. Inside, the place smells delicious. That's when I remember I haven't had anything to eat in two days. Hunger washes over me and I might as well be in a Michelin star-rated restaurant in Luxembourg. I am famished. But the thin Afghan boy preparing the food behind the stainless steel buffet counter makes me recoil in a moment of pause.

*Jesus!* I think. *Just a couple of hours ago I was about ready to get my head cut off at the hands of probably this guy's uncle. Now I am standing here in a baggy GWU sweat suit about to eat a hamburger and fries. How fucked up is my world?*

"Everything okay?" asks Ice Man.

"Fine," I reply.

I fill my tray with two burgers, two chicken breasts, and some mashed potatoes and gravy. There are plenty of other options to choose from, including a salad bar, pasta bar, baked potato station complete with every imaginable topping, and a dessert table with a chocolate fondue flowing fountain. This is definitely not your father's Vietnam. The fact that the food is this impressive, and I have yet to see anyone in a military uniform, makes me conclude that I must be on one of those secret Special Operations/Intelligence Community bases you only read about in *The New York Times*.

I take my food to a small table as Ice Man sits across from me, gripping a tall black coffee in a white Styrofoam cup.

"Paul, huh? Do you have a last name?"

"Ward. Paul A. Ward," I confess.

"And I guess the "A" stands for Asshole?" he jokes.

"Actually, it stands for Alastair. My father's name. He emigrated from Edinburg to the Polish/Scottish neighborhood of Hamtramck, Michigan, right outside Detroit, when he was just a boy.

"Interesting," he says with a skeptical look. "But I have to ask, what the heck were you doing in the FATA?"

Shit, I haven't even had one bite of my burger and the interrogation has already started.

"Well, Ice Man—actually, would you mind if I called you by a different name?"

This movie code-name thing is starting to irritate me.

"Sure, call me Val."

*Val Kilmer, the actor who played Ice Man in* Top Gun? *Is this guy for real?*

"Okay, Val, it's like this . . . "

For the next three hours I give Val/Ice Man the same data dump I had given Mr. Lincoln and his rescue team in the truck. I hold nothing back. How could I? These guys basically snatched me from certain death, and I'll be indebted to them for the rest of my life. Whatever they ask, I will not refuse. Besides, with every truthful statement I make, the more I realize what a huge prick I've been these past several years. My conscience is coming clean and I feel like repenting for all that I've done wrong.

Val looks at his watch and said, "You'd better get some rest. You've pretty much had both the worst day and best day of your life today. You've got to be tired."

"I am. But first, thank you for everything you and your men did for me today. I will never forget it."

"Hey, we gotta look out for our own over here in the hinterlands."

"And who exactly are we?" I ask.

"Come on, Paul, someone in your line of work? You know exactly who we are. We saved your ass today—just like we do every day. The difference is you're one of the few who get to see behind the curtain."

Damn, he's good! I know exactly who *they* are. I conclude that Val might make a successful international consultant himself one day. But in the meantime I thank my lucky stars he's on Uncle Sam's payroll.

He shows me out the door to a metal shipping container located directly opposite the chow hall. Inside are a simple bed and a small bathroom with toilet and shower. He instructs me to get as much sleep as I can. I thank him once again and within five minutes of my head hitting the pillow, it's lights out.

My mind churns and I start to dream . . .

*Your life was a waste. What did you accomplish? Lousy husband. Lousy father. Only the scoundrels of the underworld know of my disgraceful legacy. And now you're dead. You must be in the afterlife. But the place you find yourself in at this moment is not some heavenly utopia. Look around. All you see is pain and suffering. Evil is everywhere. You're in hell!*

I wake up sweating. It was just a nightmare, but I am still surrounded by darkness. I can't see a thing. Then I realize where I am; that windowless cargo container somewhere in the mountains of Afghanistan. I roll out of the bed and search for the door.

Sunlight immediately engulfs the room as the metal door creaks open. I have to shield my eyes from the bright intensity of day. It must be the middle of the afternoon.

*How long was I asleep?*

I'm still wearing the GWU sweats as I walk toward the chow hall. It's the only place I know to go. As my ridiculous-looking Crocs crunch across the gravel, I hear heavy metal music blaring off to my left. I look to see a half-dozen chiseled athletes training in a makeshift fitness center to AC/DC's 80's hit, "Thunder Struck." The gym is basically a covered airplane hangar packed with chin-up stations, rowing machines, medicine balls, and rusted-out barbells. One giant of a man is slamming a sledgehammer repeatedly down on a massive truck tire. I have seen this type of training before on *60 Minutes*. The men—and at least two women—are doing a cross-fit workout. This insane type of training is a combination of Olympic-style lifts coupled with gymnastics, and all performed for time. Workouts rarely last thirty minutes, yet participants easily burn 1,000 calories in that short time.

The air temperature is pushing 100 degrees and sweat is pouring off the athletes as they compete against each other in clean-and-jerk exercises with their makeshift equipment. A shirtless, bearded warrior slams down a straight bar, loaded with ungodly weight, from over his head and runs to the nearest trashcan. His head disappears beneath the rim of the can and despite the blaring music I can hear him puke. Now I know why the America has the toughest military in the world. I am intimidated just watching these guys train.

I enter the chow hall. It's packed with unshaven, tattooed heroes. They look up from their lunches and give me a disapproving stare, almost as if to say, "This is the guy who was doing business with warlords? We should have just left him."

I find the coffee machine and pour myself a large cup.

"Paul," I hear someone call.

I turn to see Abraham Lincoln sitting at a table full of his fellow warriors.

"Come here, man." He waves me over. "I want you to meet the rest of the guys."

I feel like an idiot in my outfit as I apprehensively walk over and pull up a chair.

Abraham Lincoln begins. "To start off, my real name is Pete—but you can call me Dallas." Then he points around the table and introduces me to the rest of his team, more than a dozen guys with handles like "Joker," "Outlaw," "Lumberjack," "Taco," and "Meat Loaf." I thank and shake hands with each one.

Suddenly, a large paw comes down on my shoulder. It's Val—Ice Man. He tells me I've been asleep for twelve hours and I should grab some food. I gladly oblige. For the next forty-five minutes I eat and chat with my new friends, talking about everything from their lives as special operatives to mine as a businessman.

After my meal, I follow Val into yet another shipping container. This one seems to be reinforced to withstand attack and is covered with antennas. I assume it's their command center. Once inside, he escorts me into a small conference room and tells me to wait. Within a few minutes, a young man in his early thirties enters.

This guy's different from the others. He doesn't look like a killer. Rather, he seems like someone you might stand behind in line at Starbucks. He has no visible tattoos, nor does he look like a much of an athlete. He's the first clean-shaven person I've seen at the compound. I conclude he's either an analyst or one of those elite case officers the intelligence community is always boasting about on the websites of the Central Intelligence Agency (CIA), Defense Intelligence Agency (DIA), or some other three-letter alphabet soup organization.

He stands across from where I'm sitting and drops a thick manila folder on the table—just like in a bad cop show.

"So, you're a Michigan man."

"That's right. Go Blue!"

"Go fuck yourself," he coldly replies. "I went to Michigan State."

Great! An MSU Spartan. Michigan's in-state rival. Michigan State is that institution of higher learning that *Playboy* once ranked as the best party school in America. The super-secret, covert operations squad must have had an opening on their party-planning committee. I'm sure this clown tells some great stories around the bonfire about funneling beer and banging sorority girls.

"So, that's how you got assigned here instead of Rome?" I joke, trying to keep things civilized.

"No, I'm here because I want to make a difference."

"Sure," I respond smugly. "And I bet your call sign is Spartan," I quip, citing the MSU mascot.

"As matter of fact, it is. But that's not important. What's important is your future."

*Oh shit! Here it comes.* "Sparty" here is about to threaten me.

"You see, Mr. Ward, you've broken the law of just about every country on Earth. But what really pisses me off is that you conspired against the United States of America."

"Wait a second!" I fire back. "I did nothing of the kind!"

"Bullshit! You're a traitor, and if I can prove it I'm gonna see you hanged for it."

"Listen to me. You may despise who and what I am. And that's fine. But you and I have two very important things in common. One, we deal with shit bags for a living, and two, we both love our country. I just happen to make a lot more money at it."

"Save the speech for your attorney, tough guy."

"What, you think I just got off the boat? You and I are alone in this room right now. No Ice Man around. You're trying to play the bad cop with your ridiculous folder, your insults, and your threats. So, cut the shit. What's the real story here?"

"Are you willing to help your country in return for your freedom?"

I stare at him for a moment. "Let's say for the moment that I am willing. What do I have to do?"

Sparty reaches into the manila folder and pulls out a photo.

"The French Intelligence service recruited a woman about a year ago to help catch one of her boyfriends, a known arms smuggler. Turns out you stumbled across their radar instead."

He drops the photo on the table, a full-color picture of Lola going into her apartment building in Paris.

"Shit!" I say under my breath.

"When they discovered you were using multiple passports, they decided they'd sit back and watch what exactly you were up to. After your escapades in Africa and the Middle East, they shared the information with us."

"But you didn't know my true identity."

"Correct. We weren't really sure of your actual name or real nationality. It's just a nice coincidence you're American. In fact, when you showed up in Dubai on your Italian passport, we were ready to turn the case over to the Carabinieri. But then you received a phone call from the arms dealer known as the Sheik, who we had under surveillance. That's how you came across my desk. Hell, I even sat right next to you on the flight from Rome to Dubai—not that you noticed. We then tracked your cell phone by overhead drone and that led us right to you in that Afghan cave."

*Holy shit, this guy was the idiot who was sitting right next to me on the plane a few days ago!*

I feel like I have been played for a complete fool. It is the first time this has ever happened in my career. Damn it! I can't let on that he played me.

"Impressive, but couldn't you guys have shown up a little bit sooner? I was seconds away from being a head shorter."

"You're alive, aren't you?" he said flatly. "And now you have nice GWU sweat suit to show for it, Michigan man."

"What about Yuri?" I ask.

"Who's Yuri?"

I start to laugh. Unless this guy is lying to me, which in all likelihood is possible, Yuri isn't on the USG's radar.

"Sparty, you're an alright guy, and I do remember you from the airplane. Although, you do play a forgettable seatmate well. And, all kidding aside, thank you for saving my ass. You don't have to threaten me with anything. I'm in your debt. Just tell me what you need me to do."

He takes out another picture from the folder and slaps it down in front me. It is a familiar face, which I recognize immediately.

"Mr. Ward, we need you to go to South America and kill a dictator."

# DICTATORS
## IV

# ASSASSINATE

*Location: Dubai, UAE*
*Time: 2133 hours*

I'm trying to relax in the Emirates Business Lounge at Dubai International Airport. The Michigan State Spartan, whom I've learned calls himself Joe, is sitting across from me and pretending we're not traveling together. We've just flown in from Islamabad, Pakistan, after a connecting flight through Kabul. We took a helicopter from our undisclosed location to Afghanistan's capital city. Joe is apparently keeping tabs on me. He said others are watching me too and that I should simply play the part of a businessman and "not do anything stupid, like to try make a run for it."

I have no intention of testing him. Besides, I'm back in my element. I'm in an airport business lounge, and Joe even managed to provide me with a fitted suit from Pakistan—though it's made of cheap fabric and hangs on me like cardboard.

The last three weeks have been a blur. I've essentially spent every waking hour being briefed by various intelligence community operatives about my new assignment for the US Intelligence Community—killing a dictator.

Each of the men and women with whom I've been in contact specializes in a different field of expertise. Some excel at understanding Latin American politics, while others know terrorism and narco-trafficking better than anyone I've ever met. A handful of them are analysts with PhDs. Some of the technical guys remind me of the jack-of-all-trade character MacGyver from the '80s television series. I also met a psychiatrist and a chemist. All of them have served the same purpose, which is to educate me about my target—the Latin American tyrant I will refer to only as "Don Pedro."

Dictators are an interesting breed. I should know. I've worked with quite a few over the years. The late Kim Jung Il, and now his son Kim Jong Un, are undoubtedly the reigning champs of dictatorships. Fortunately, I never had to do business with either of them. Saddam Hussein was a helluva dictator as well. He ruled Iraq with an iron fist; killing some thirty thousand of his people every year, apparently just to keep everyone in check. Nevertheless, I'm sure many people—even in the United States—wish we could turn back the clock to return Saddam to power, thereby avoiding the chaos that has ensued following the 2003 invasion.

It's funny; Saddam was a slow-paying client of mine before the second Gulf War. Surprised? Who do you think brokered all those oil-for-money deals on the black market? Then, after the US Army swept into Baghdad and deposed Saddam, I amassed a small fortune in commissions by hiding money in Swiss bank accounts for the newly installed—and thoroughly corrupt—post-Saddam government. That puppet administration skimmed money faster than a bartender at strip club.

To be honest, it was some of the easiest money I ever made. I feel guilty about it now, but compared to the billions of dollars that large defense contractors and logistics supply companies earned from Operation Enduring Freedom, it just proved how prophetic President Dwight D. Eisenhower was when he warned of the dangers of the military-industrial complex.

This time I'm getting paid with my freedom in exchange for doing a dirty job. I kill Don Pedro and they let me walk away. Despite the assurances, I've got a pit in my stomach telling me somehow this new engagement isn't going to turn out well.

I won't reveal the true identity of Don Pedro, or the country in Latin America over which he presides. But I will tell you this: the man deserves to die. As Clint Eastwood famously said in the movie *Unforgiven*, "We all have it coming."

Don Pedro assumed power in a military coup several years

ago. He quickly installed a military junta, which he claimed was a "socialist movement meant to bring equality to all men and women, particularly by lifting the poor up into the middle class." By seizing control of the country's natural resources and nationalizing all private utilities—including foreign-owned companies—Don Pedro ended up controlling 90 percent of the nation's GDP. As one of his first official presidential acts, he declared himself President for Life. He also immediately installed his military cronies in cabinet positions, and he executed—without trial—all of the members of the previous government.

To make matters worse, the new government's lack of understanding of economics and foreign policy thrust the country deeply into debt with the World Bank and the International Monetary Fund. Don Pedro's increasingly poor human rights record isolated him further. The country has been suspended numerous times by the Organization of American States.

Despite these setbacks, Don Pedro has become one of the wealthiest men in the hemisphere, second only to Mexican telecom tycoon Carlos Slim. His net worth is believed to be in the billions, though most of it is hidden in offshore accounts in the Cayman Islands and other tax havens. Don Pedro is married with children, but his sexual appetite is renowned throughout Latin America. It is reputed that he has slept with at least one different woman each week since he took power. If so, only the late Wilt Chamberlain existed in more rarified territory.

To further enhance his already devious resume, Don Pedro also sells weapons on the black market to countries sanctioned by the United Nations for supporting terrorism. There are two daily, direct flights from the capital of his country to Tehran. The cargo and passenger manifests are unknown. Most analysts think he is moving a combination of military weapons, kidnapped Latin women to be used as sex slaves, gold, and possibly even uranium extracted from his country's mines. No wonder the US government wants him dead. Although I find it disheartening, I recognize that I'm their most viable option to achieve that goal.

You might not believe this, but I've killed people before. I didn't like doing it, and I'm certainly not a professional killer. But there have been times when the wrong person crossed my path and had to be eliminated. Who they were or how I did it isn't important. I admit I'm not proud of it, but I've never lost any sleep over it, either. It was part of the job. So, I will feel no remorse killing a man notorious for repressing and torturing thousands of his own citizens for his own personal gain.

My method of assassination will be slow-acting poison. My handlers—Joe in particular—have provided me with a quick-dissolving powder concealed inside a pair of silver cufflinks. The pearl in the center of each cufflink swings open and will allow me to drop the powder into Don Pedro's drinking glass as I reach above it. With two cufflinks come two chances. As the covert operations community wholeheartedly believes, two is one and one is none. Joe's medical colleagues also claim the powder will leave no evidence. Any doctor performing the autopsy will be convinced the cause of death was a brain aneurism. It also doesn't take effect until forty-eight hours after consumption, allowing me plenty of time to escape.

All I'll have to do is persuade Don Pedro to take me on as a political adviser. I'll use my international consultant reputation as a calling card, which should allow me to get close enough to him to poison his drink. It's ironic. I just had my ass saved by the finest killing machines the US government has at its disposal, people requiring years and millions of dollars to train. But instead of using men like Mr. Lincoln, they have opted to have me eliminate this dictator.

*No, this plan doesn't stink of shit at all!*

\* \* \*

I look up from my newspaper and see Joe typing on his MacBook Air. I have a feeling he isn't emailing his wife. Rather, he's probably filing a report to his own handlers. Glancing around the lounge, I see several large men who don't appear too comfortable wearing their government-issued black suits. They're obviously Joe's not-so-clandestine backup team. I find it strangely reassuring he wasn't lying to me. I also like the fact that there are a few extra pairs of eyes watching my back. Despite escaping from the warlord Pasha, I still fear Yuri—and numerous other disgruntled business colleagues from my past.

No. Despite the slight reassurances, this plan sucks, and our travel itinerary is sloppy. I would never operate in this manner. If I did, I wouldn't have been able to stay in business for so long. Now I know why I've been contracted for this assignment. They need a good consultant just as much as the various shady characters with whom I normally deal.

I reach into my briefcase to consult General Sun Tzu. He at least never disappoints me. Turing to a random page, I am filled with the following ironic wisdom:

*There is no country that has benefited from prolonged warfare.*

The ancient author of *The Art of War* has struck the nail on the head, as always. In Vietnam, Iraq, Afghanistan, and even the Global War on Terrorism, maybe America has finally realized that fighting a long, messy war is pointless and wasteful when the objective is to cut off the head of the snake.

Think Osama bin Laden, Muammar Gaddafi, or Saddam Hussein; all dead but the mess remains. Forget nation building. Forget boots on the ground. Forget drone strikes, for that matter. This is not national security. One neat little pill can take the place of billions of dollars spent and thousands of lives lost. And best of all, the President of the United States can address the nation and say, "This bad man is dead and no American lives were lost in the process." That's considered a victory in today's highly politically correct world.

What happens if I get caught? Who cares? I am totally expendable, and the US intelligence community retains plausible deniability because of my criminal background. I realize that, for the first time in my life, I sound like the wacky conspiracy theorists. If this assignment goes wrong, the history books could be debating my involvement as an assassin much like Lee Harvey Oswald. In other words, I'm fucked. My stomach begins to churn and I have to excuse myself to the toilet.

"Excuse me, sir. Would you mind watching my bags while I use the restroom?" I ask Joe, pretending we don't know each other.

"Of course," he replies, playing the stranger.

As I walk to the men's room, I see the surveillance team suddenly perk up. They start nodding to one another around the lounge. But I'm not the only one to see it. A couple of Arab gentlemen, dressed in expensive suits, take notice as well and begin whispering to each other. My stomach is too queasy for me to care. I head into the men's room and into a vacant stall. Lifting the toilet seat, I vomit bile in one heaving lurch. I wipe my mouth with the back of my hand and perch over the bowl on both knees. How did it come to this?

After my pit stop, I collect my thoughts and attempt to regain my composure. Now standing in front of the bathroom sink, I splash some cold water on my face and rinse out my mouth. I look at myself again in the mirror and tell the person staring back at me, "You're still the man!"

I walk back out into the lounge more confident, and see the surveillance team still hopping around like jackrabbits. I doubt these particular guys will ever succeed in the private sector when they retire from government service. Luckily, they'll receive a nice pension.

I sit back down across from Joe and give him a cursory "thank you" for watching my bags.

"Not a problem," he calmly replies.

I decide I need to bust his balls a little. I notice the green, block letter S displayed prominently on the luggage tag of his computer bag. Pretending we're still strangers, I point to his bag and ask, "Did you graduate from Michigan State?"

Startled at my remark, Joe nervously replies, "Yes, I did."

"Really, I went to the University of Michigan," I continue.

"Small world," he quips, obviously annoyed.

Continuing my ruse, I ask, "You know what Michigan State graduates call University of Michigan graduates, don't you?"

Joe's not happy, but plays along anyway. "No."

"Boss," I say with a smug grin.

Now visibly pissed off, Joe snaps his laptop shut and stuffs it into his bag. Then he gets up and stomps off to the espresso machine. He must be tired of me.

If I'm going to be a patsy, I might as well have fun doing it. Besides, this guy is more of a pain-in-the-ass than a suitcase with no handles. I enjoy pissing him off.

The public-address system blares an announcement: "Flight 123 for São Paulo, Brazil, now boarding at Gate 45."

I gather up my belongings and walk toward the gate. Joe and the surveillance team are in tow, ten steps behind me. I'm off to dupe a dictator into hiring me.

# LUCKY 13

*Location:* São Paulo, Brazil
*Time:* 0937 hours

"*Bom dia,*" the striking female immigration officer greets me, as I hand her my Brazilian passport at Guarulhos International Airport.

"*Bom dia,*" I respond. "*Tudo bom?*"

"*Sim, tudo bem.*"

With that simple exchange of pleasantries I have entered Brazil, my favorite country in South America.

Joe, aka "Sparty," my handler, has dragged me halfway across the globe from Afghanistan in order to finalize the details of our operation against the soon-to-be assassinated Latin American dictator in a nearby country known as *Don Pedro.*

Known for its vibrant, fun-loving people, Brazil is a nation that has never quite realized its economic potential. It's almost like one of those football stars drafted right out of college in the first round, and years later the fans are still wondering when he'll finally live up to the hype. Likewise, the international community is still waiting for Brazil's breakthrough moment. Adopting three different currencies over the past three decades, not to mention suffering under a dictatorship for twenty years, Brazil still has a long way to go.

I've been traveling to this immensely diverse nation of 200 million citizens for several years. I spent much of my youth down here surfing along the many unspoiled beaches of Florianopolis, a large island off the coast, as well as learning to play "the beautiful game," aka *futebol*—or soccer as they say in America. But that story I will not share with you. It's too personal. Yes, back in Afghanistan I revealed my entire life to my rescuers. Still, there are things you need not know. But I digress.

When most people think of Brazil, they think of the sexy flavor of Copacabana Beach, the excitement of Carnaval, enchanting bossa nova music like "Águas de Março," and the breeding ground from which Victoria's Secret models hail. Coincidently, I once sat across the aisle from Brazilian supermodel Gisele Bundchen on a flight from Miami to Rio. She was even more beautiful in person. Though she never looked in my direction, it pleased me to know she ended up marrying a fellow University of Michigan graduate—NFL star quarterback Tom Brady of the New England Patriots.

My early years in Florianopolis are not the reason I possess a genuine Brazilian passport. I earned that perk by helping the government of former President Luiz Inácio Lula da Silva secure the rights to host both the World Cup and the Olympics. It took a lot of backdoor dealings. Unfortunately for the Lula administration, most of their team, including a certain chief of staff, were later indicted on corruption charges and imprisoned.

Before all of that happened, I managed to help move much of the funds from one secret international account to another. It wasn't that difficult. When you reach a certain level of power, the normal checks and balances in government become much less enforceable. In fact, it is harder to wire transfer $50,000 from the US to Brazil than it is to transfer $50 million from Brazil to the Cayman Islands.

I performed what I consider my finest work for the state-owned oil giant. Talk about a difficult assignment! My ability to slice off billions of dollars worth of kickbacks to corrupt Brazilian politicians should have earned me the Nobel Prize in economics. People say Warren Buffet is a financial genius, but I'd love to see him try to hide five billion dollars.

\* \* \*

São Paulo is the economic hub of Latin America. Although Rio de Janeiro is much more popular as a tourist destination, São Paulo is the engine that drives Brazil. A metropolis three times the size of New York City and boasting a population of 21 million residents, São Paulo has some of the world's worst traffic. So gridlocked are its roads that most high-level executives travel from meeting to meeting via helicopters positioned on the roofs of the numerous corporate towers. These air taxis pockmark the ever-expanding skyline daily, appearing like a swarm of flies to the people on the busy streets below. In fact, São Paulo has the most helicopters per square kilometer than any other city in the world—as well as armored cars, due to the high crime rates.

Also of interest, São Paulo is an eclectic city, boasting the largest Italian, Japanese, and Lebanese populations outside of those countries. It means the city is a culinary destination to which foodies travel from the four corners of the planet. If you can't find it in São Paulo, it probably doesn't exist.

But be warned, São Paulo can be daunting. As the Paulistanos are fond of saying, "São Paulo is not for amateurs." That is exactly why I like it down here. The ability of the police to apprehend criminals is a paltry 2 percent. I can easily vanish among a sea of millions. Why do you think so many Nazis escaped to Brazil and Argentina after World War II? Hell, Hitler's mad scientist, Joseph Mengele—who was thought to be already dead during the Nuremberg Trials—was living on a coffee farm in the Bertioga beachtown in São Paulo state when he died.

Incidentally, it was always reported that Mengele had drowned when he suffered a stroke while swimming in the ocean off the coast. Truth be told, Mossad, the powerful Israeli intelligence service, sent a team of scuba divers to swim up underneath him and pull him under until his lungs filled with seawater. An old Mossad agent named Ari told me the story one night over too many bottles of Manischewitz in Tel Aviv. Ari claimed he was the first member of the team to grab Mengele's ankles, while Mengele floated casually on his back in the Brazilian surf.

Anyway, every time I return to this magnificent city, I am sure to stay at the Emiliano Hotel, a few blocks down from the famous Avenida Paulista in the posh neighborhood of Jardins.

I also make it a point to eat *polpettone*, a unique breaded hamburger baked in tomato sauce and Parmesan cheese at the quaint Jardim de Napoli Restaurant.

But this isn't a pleasure trip. My handlers are directing my movements, and I must play by their rules. My buddy Joe is up my ass 24/7, and I honestly think he's enjoying his role too much. In my humble opinion, the guy's a complete dick. I've decided that my behavior toward him is to be polite, but obfuscate.

Joe and I breeze through customs at Guarulhos and pass through the automatic doors into the arrivals terminal. There is a huge mob of people, many of them private drivers holding up signs with passenger names, all standing behind a steel security fence that looks like an oversized bicycle rack. Scanning the crowd, a casually dressed, middle-aged gentleman in a white linen shirt grabs Sparty's attention. He presses against the edge of the guardrail waving an arm.

"Joe!" the man yells over the chaos.

"Jack! How the hell are you, amigo? It's been a long time!"

The two men hug across the barrier as if they haven't seen each other in years.

"Same shit, different shithole," the man replies.

Joe gives him a sly grin and continues. "Come on, you know you love it here. I bet you have at least two *namoradas* walking around your apartment in skimpy Brazilian bikinis every weekend."

The man smiles. "Okay, you got me."

Still separated by the barricade, Joe introduces me.

"Jack, I want you to meet my friend, Paul."

Jack shakes my hand and begins pumping it up and down.

"Hi Paul, I'm Jack, the chief in São Paulo. Damn glad to meet you. You're a hard man to keep up with. It will be a pleasure working with you for once instead of against you."

"The pleasure's all mine," I reply stoically.

We make our way out to the parking lot and toward Jack's vehicle, a black, Level-III armored, Kia Sportage SUV. Armored vehicles are not uncommon in São Paulo, where carjackings occur every fifteen minutes. Anyone who's anyone drives an armored car, especially the local station chief.

"So, where are we headed?" I naively ask.

"Safehouse," Joe tells me in a stern voice, as if I'm not supposed to be asking any questions.

We drive for nearly 90 minutes, most of it sitting in traffic. Eventually, we come to an urban neighborhood with twisting streets and graffiti covering the majority of the tall apartment buildings. Each building sits behind a razor wire fence with an armed guard sitting in a shack just inside the fence line. Prostitutes in skimpy skirts adorn the street corners—even though it's midday.

We pull up to the gates of one of the random buildings, and Jack gives two quick beeps of his horn. The guard in his glass booth looks up from his paper, recognizes Jack, and opens the automatic gate, which slides on its track. We pull forward into a tight parking garage. Jack finds an empty spot in the dank building and turns off the vehicle.

"We're here," he says.

"Where?" I ask.

"Our command center," he replies.

"Sounds exciting."

Joe turns around in the passenger seat and shoots me a look, which says "shut the hell up before I beat your ass."

I just smile, which I know pisses him off.

The three of us file into the compact garage elevator. I am closest to the buttons.

"Hit 13, Paul," Jack instructs me.

The thirteenth floor is at the top of a rundown apartment complex.

"I hope you're not superstitious," he continues.

"Are you kidding?" I respond, "Dan Marino (who wore number 13 on his jersey) was my favorite quarterback when I was kid. Now it's Tom Brady. You know who he is, right, Joe?"

"Fuck you," Joe says, without looking in my direction.

The elevator opens, and we walk down a damp hallway to a door marked 1307A. It's at the end of the corridor and there is a tiny camera angled down from above the doorframe. Joe knocks four times—two knocks, a one second pause, and two more knocks. The door creaks open, and we quickly file in.

I am stunned by the complexity of what I see. Inside are television monitors hanging on the walls that remind me of

NASA's control center in Houston. There are also half a dozen twenty-somethings typing away feverishly on their MacBook laptops. I suspect these geeky-looking youngsters specialize in hacking the emails of others.

"Welcome to our command center," says Jack.

"Holy shit! You weren't kidding," I say in awe.

"We have everything we need in here to monitor cell phones, conduct drone strikes, manage coups—even kill dictators," Jack jokes.

I'm not sure how much of that is true. But I do start to feel the weight of an impending storm.

Joe puts his hand on my shoulder, as if to remind me that this is all for real.

"You'd better not fuck up," he whispers.

Jack senses my uneasiness and tries to calm my nerves.

"Paul," he says, "Why don't you go take a hot shower and lie down for a bit? You must be tired after your flight. There's a bedroom in the back just for you. I need to speak with Joe here, and we'll wake you up in a couple hours and go grab something to eat."

I conclude that Jack is a seasoned intelligence officer who has used his easygoing demeanor to reassure many an asset before sending them off in dangerous operations. I decide to oblige and head to the back bedroom to relax for a couple hours.

After a hot shower, I crawl into the full-size bed. I must admit it's a welcome relief after nearly a month trying to sleep in Afghanistan. The room is dark and the air conditioner hums a soothing tune. Cold air blows on me while I stretch out under the crisp, clean sheets. Within a few minutes, I am fast asleep.

# OPERATION CONSULTOR

**Location:** *A Safe House*
**Time:** *Unknown*

I open my eyes. I don't know where I am. I'm lying on my stomach with my ear pressed against the pillow. A face comes into view of my blurred vision.

"Rise and shine, asshole!"

Startled by the sudden interruption, my heartbeat accelerates. Joe's come to wake me from my nap, and he seems to enjoy the fact that he scared me. I'm surprised he didn't dump a bucket of cold water on my head.

"Do you actually plan on doing something worthwhile, or should we stop wasting everyone's time and just send you to a Supermax prison right now?"

"I'm up," I say, not wishing to get further into this bullshit banter.

"I told Jack, as well as everyone at Langley who would listen, that you were a piece of garbage and that we'd be better off conducting a PSYOP campaign to oust Don Pedro rather than risk using your selfish ass. You know what he told me? He said you were nothing more than a commodity to be used and that even if you shit the bed on this operation, we're prepared to move forward with multiple contingency plans right behind you. So my friend, just remember, you get one shot at this. If you fuck up, you'll vanish into a dark hole, and nobody will ever hear from you again. Not your family, not your friends, not all those skanks you have scattered around the globe. No more tailored suits, no more gourmet meals. One prison uniform and oatmeal for the rest of your life."

This was not the way I expected to wake up. Maybe I underestimated Joe. Maybe he's a better operative than I initially thought. Either way, he's right; this is my only shot at freedom. As much as I'd prefer not to be in this situation, failure is not an option. I must kill Don Pedro. And even then I still wouldn't be certain I'd actually be released. I find myself in the unfamiliar situation of having to trust others. I find myself having to trust the United States government.

After Joe's little pep talk, I walk out of the bedroom into the command center. Jack and the team of whiz kids are working away like beavers.

"Get dressed," Jack instructs. "We're going to meet your partner."

"My partner?" I say, caught off guard. "We never talked about a partner. I work alone."

"Things have changed. Headquarters doesn't want you acting within the country without a minder."

"A minder?" I protest. "This is what I do for a living. I've made millions at this job—alone—because I'm the best at this shit!"

"You're the best at consulting for dictators," Jack shoots back. "You're not the best when it comes to assassinations. So we've brought in someone to help you through the particular challenges of the assignment."

"Jesus H. Christ! You people are really something. I've worked with illiterate tribesmen in the heart of Africa who eat monkey brains for breakfast that were better organized than you."

"Knock it off and get dressed."

"How about letting me go out and buy some new clothes?"

"Not a chance," Joe snaps. "We turn you loose on the streets of São Paulo and we'll never see you again. Put on the suit we got you in Pakistan."

"Seriously? You expect me to wear that burlap sack again? Guys, I recognize that dot-gov lifers such as yourselves do all your suit shopping at Men's Warehouse, but in the international business community, if I show up in that polyester getup you picked out for me, I'll be shot on sight."

"Shut the fuck up," Joe replies. "You can buy some clothes with your new partner before the consulate party."

"What consulate party?"

"You and your new partner have been invited to the residence of the consul general from Don Pedro's country tonight," Jack says. "You'll be attending as your partner's escort. Once inside, you'll cozy up the consul general—who's Don Pedro's half-brother—and persuade him to set a face-to-face meeting with El Presidente, which is how you'll dispense your little gift to him."

"This isn't what we discussed in Afghanistan."

Jack calmly replies, "Paul, did you really think that we would tell you the exact details of our operation that far in advance?"

"Why do I get the feeling you just made up these plans on the spot?"

Ever cool, Jack says, "Maybe we did, maybe we didn't. What's important now is that it's show time. Now, go get dressed."

* * *

I often say there are three things a man should never wear: Capri pants, a fanny pack, and a Speedo "banana hammock" bathing suit. But Brazilians break all three rules. They even insist on carrying those godawful selfie sticks with them when they travel. Now I have a fourth item to add to my list: a suit from Pakistan. Wearing this thing I feel like some refugee fresh off the boat.

We arrive at the Sky Bar, high atop Hotel Unique in the Jardim Paulista neighborhood. Hotel Unique is just that—unique—because it takes the shape of a giant half-watermelon.

We're here to meet my new partner, who according to Joe and Jack, is a true professional who knows how to behave among dictators and other nefarious characters.

We make our way through the fashionable crowd, which can only be described as São Paulo's sexiest people. Jack and Joe sport their $199 government suits with scuffed up loafers resembling orthopedic shoes, while I follow in tow in my Borat costume. You don't have to be fluent in Portuguese to know that the ever-so-hip Paulistanos are rolling their eyes and muttering "stupid gringos" under their breath. If I were here alone, I would be able to blend in as a local. Right now, we might as well be wearing WE'RE WITH THE US GOVERNMENT signs around our necks.

We head through the bar towards the glass balcony, which overlooks the immense city skyline. At our feet is a narrow swimming pool, sunk into the balcony floor, lined with bright red tiles and illuminated by underwater lights. I've been here at 3 a.m. sometimes when beautiful young Brazilian girls strip down to their lingerie and drunkenly dive in. May we'll be lucky like that tonight. It sure would break up the monotony of hanging out with these two tools.

The bright lights of the tall buildings in the distance immediately remind me of New York City, and suddenly I wish I were in the Big Apple instead of São Paulo. Then something—rather someone—changes my mind. Standing alone along the glass railing is one of the most stunning women I have ever seen. She is so indescribably gorgeous I gasp as if a boxer has punched me in the gut and momentarily deprived me of oxygen. She is tall and tan, young and lovely—the Girl from Ipanema in the flesh—and is wearing a sequined red dress. Her curly brunette hair hangs down over her exposed and toned back and shoulders. Her long legs seem to go on for days. For the first time in my life, I finally understand when people talk about love at first sight.

Joe is apparently saying something to me. I see his lips moving in my peripheral vision, but I have completely tuned him out. I can't stop gawking at this gorgeous woman.

"Asshole. Hey, asshole!" Joe barks.

"What?" I bark back.

"It's time to meet your partner, dipshit."

The two men from the government begin to walk towards this goddess. *Holy shit! They're actually going to talk to her.* Suddenly I feel like a teenager again, and my chums are going to tell the most popular girl in the school that I like her. What the fuck is happening?

Jack, the ever coolheaded intelligence chief, begins to speak. "Paul Ward, I would like you to meet your new partner, Mariana Ribeiro Motta."

Extending my hand, I try to play it cool. On the inside I think I was less nervous when the Taliban had a knife to my neck.

"*Muito prazer, Senhorita Motta,*" I say nervously.

The amazing woman's full lips open as she smiles wide. Her exposed teeth are equally perfect.

"*Muito bom, Senhor Ward.* You speak Portuguese! It is a pleasure to meet you as well. Please call me Mariana," she says in the most sensual of accents.

It's official. I'm in love. I even start to feel an erection building in my ridiculous, made-in-Islamabad trousers. Now I really feel like I'm in high school.

Joe chimes in, just to ensure that I don't get too friendly.

"Mariana, don't let this professional bullshit artist fool you. He's a manipulative bastard who's also a traitor to his country."

"Thanks for the vote of confidence," I say with a scowl.

"I'm a big girl, Joe," Mariana responds. "I can handle myself, thank you."

Joe appears embarrassed, as if he regrets his last words, while I find myself even more smitten.

"Maybe we should find a table and order some drinks?" Jack says.

Soon thereafter, the four of us are sitting at a corner table in the bar, away from the blaring lounge music. We each order a *caipirinha*, the traditional Brazilian rum-like drink made of *cachaça*, sugar, and muddled limes. Mariana orders a slight variation by ordering a caipiroska, in which vodka replaces the *cachaça*. When the waiter asks her what kind of vodka she prefers, she says "Grey Goose." Using this as a chance to be charming, I throw out an old joke.

"Grey Goose," I say, "good choice."

"Thank you," Mariana replies.

"You know why Hitler never drank vodka, don't you?"

"Here it comes," interrupts Joe.

"No," Mariana replies, leaning in closer to me, enough for me to catch the fragrance of her hair. "Why did Hitler never drink vodka?"

I move in ever closer to her face and say in a soft voice, "Because it made him mean."

"God, you're such a loser!" Joe snaps. "It's amazing that you've ever gotten laid in your life."

I ignore Joe and continue to look into Mariana's eyes. She is giggling, though I don't know if she's laughing at the joke or at me. Either way, I'm starting to feel more confident. I also want her more than ever.

My joke has also fallen flat on Jack, so he decides it's time to get down to business.

"Paul, let's get serious. As I told you back at the safe house, your assignment is to attend the party tonight with Mariana at the home of the consul general. Your objective is to meet with him, whose name is Rodrigo Hernandez. He's the half-brother of Don Pedro, and should he like you, he'll recommend that you have an audience with the President. Hernandez has a bit of a crush on Mariana, so it should be easy to get close to him."

"Who wouldn't have a crush on Mariana?" I say.

"Idiot," Joe snaps. I'm detecting a whiff of jealousy.

Mariana smiles and Jack continues. "Mariana, whose cover is that of a corrupt, chief political strategist within the Brazilian presidential administration, is going to offer Hernandez a deal to take to his brother. Essentially, Brazil will provide millions of gallons worth of free oil, which Don Pedro can sell for profit any way he sees fit. In return, Don Pedro agrees to support some bullshit Organization of American States resolution about protecting the Amazon Rainforest.

"This is a no-brainer for Don Pedro. Mariana, you'll introduce Paul as the middleman who'll handle the logistics of the deal and provide the necessary protection from media and international scrutiny. For this reason, it is imperative that Paul—and Paul alone—be allowed to have dinner with Don Pedro in order to explain the proper cover mechanisms that are needed. Because Paul is technically an international consultant, there will be nothing suspicious about him meeting privately with Don Pedro to discuss the political strategy. While Paul is alone with Don Pedro, he must find a way to drop the poison into his drink or onto his food. If all goes to plan, Don Pedro will be dead within two weeks, and the cause of death will be found to have been a brain aneurysm. If and when that happens, we'll let Paul get on an airplane and disappear back into his life."

"Sounds like a clean and easy plan to me," Joe says.

"Bullshit! There's no such thing as a clean and easy plan," I counter.

"Then just don't fuck up," Joe huffs.

"That's enough," Jack snaps. "Everyone just put your personal feelings aside and do your job. All of our necks are on the line, not just Paul's. If this thing goes south, it'll be a media shit storm and then we'll all be hung out to dry. It's an all or nothing game. That's why we brought Paul into this. In twenty years, he's always come through."

"Except in Afghanistan—just saying," Joe cracks.

"Regardless, this plan must succeed. Failure is not an option," Jack says.

"Jack is correct," Mariana says, jumping in. "If word of this gets out, it won't just be Don Pedro's country that the US will have to worry about. The relationship between the United States and Brazil will also be damaged for years to come."

"So that's it, then," I calmly say. "Failure is not an option."

The waiter returns to our table with our drinks. He flirts with Mariana as he sets her drink down first. As the waiter leaves, I note that hint of jealousy in Joe again. No question, he's got a thing for her as well.

Jack lifts his glass in a toast and says, "To Operation Consultor."

The rest of us clink our glasses and repeat, "To Operation Consultor."

The samba music is getting louder, and the bar is filling up with more attractive Brazilians. Little do any of these people know that the four individuals sitting in the corner—three bland-looking men and one gorgeous woman—have just kicked off a plot to assassinate a South American dictator.

# THE RECEPTION

**Location:** *The Consulate*
**Time:** *2110 hours*

I'm riding with Mariana as she drives her silver, armored Ford Fusion to the consulate and our anticipated meeting with the consul general, Rodrigo Hernandez. We said goodbye to Jack and Sparty at the bar. They are headed back to the safe house to anxiously await our report later in the evening. As Mariana negotiates the insane São Paulo traffic, I focus on how to talk to this stunningly beautiful woman alone.

"So, Mariana," I begin, "How did you come to work with these guys?"

"My husband," she replies. Those two words immediately deflate me. *She's married. Shit!*

"Does your husband work for them, too?"

"No," she replies. "My husband is dead."

*Yes, yes, yes!* "My God, I'm sorry, Mariana."

"You should be," she bites back.

"I'm sorry. I didn't mean to pry."

"My husband was in the military. He fought in Afghanistan with the Army's 82nd Airborne. He was killed by a roadside bomb, eight years ago, by the Taliban."

As she pauses, I know what's coming.

"The same Taliban you were doing business with, you bastard! The same Taliban you supplied with weapons to kill US troops!"

Her eyes begin to tear up, ever so slightly, but she gracefully maintains her composure, while I feel like a total heel.

"Mariana, I'm sorry. Please know, I wasn't the one selling weapons to the Taliban. It was the Russians. I was just there to monitor the delivery man."

"Sure. You know what, I should pull out my gun right now and stick a bullet in your head!"

*Shit! No, no, no.* Mariana despises me—though I wonder if she's really concealing a handgun.

"You're right; I am guilty," I said quietly. "But Mariana, if I could undo my mistakes, I would. I don't expect you to understand, much less forgive me, but know that I am sorry for my actions. Maybe by killing Don Pedro I can redeem some of my past actions."

A few moments of silence. Then Mariana, perhaps trying to put me in my place or just get it off her chest, continues.

"I met my husband on Ipanema Beach. He was backpacking through Brazil after college. I had just finished with my university studies in São Paulo and was in Rio on holiday. We fell in love immediately. A year later, I moved up to Miami with him. We married a year later. Then September 11th happened. My husband, being a patriotic American, volunteered for the military and did multiple tours in both Iraq and Afghanistan. He promised me he was going to quit, but he kept going back, because he couldn't stop until the job was finished. Then he was killed instantly when his Humvee drove over an IED in Kandahar."

"I'm sorry," I say, and this time I mean it.

"I felt sorry for myself for about a year. Then I decided I needed to do something that would make my husband proud and preserve his memory. So, I found my way into these covert operations."

She unexpectedly starts laughing. "I renounced my Brazilian citizenship and tried to pick up where my husband left off. I wanted to be posted in the Middle East or Central Asia, but my language skills and area knowledge of South America landed me in the Latin America Division. Now, here I am, working with you to kill this slimy dictator. Some legacy to keep for my husband."

"Jesus, Mariana, you're an amazing woman."

"Fuck you."

"You're right," I say. "Fuck me, indeed."

At that moment, Mariana jerks the steering wheel hard to the left, jumping the median. All four of the vehicle's wheels leave the pavement. When the car slams back to the ground, she turns a hard right and jumps us back into our original lane. The car never slows down for a second.

"What the hell was that?" I sputter.

"Sorry about that. Two men on a motorcycle on our left side were about to carjack us," she says calmly.

"What?"

"It happens all the time here. One guy drives the motorcycle while the guy on the back points a gun and demands you to pull over. As soon as I saw the gun, I ran them off the road. We're safe now."

"Are we?"

Mariana smiles. I think she's enjoyed that moment of excitement to take her mind off her husband.

We continue driving in silence for another twenty minutes until we pull up to the front gate of the consulate.

"We're here," is all she says to me.

Brandishing our gold-foiled invitation to a security guard, we make our way through a large wrought-iron gate onto a beautiful driveway lined with gray brick pavers. The consulate itself is an old-fashioned, Portuguese-inspired townhouse that looks over 200 years old. Small white bulbs, resembling Christmas lights, are strung throughout the many palm trees and illuminate the well-manicured lawn. Two Afro-descendent valets in bright red jackets simultaneously open our doors. I briefly take a look at the left side of the car and notice that there is no evidence of any damage from our encounter with the carjackers. Then again, why would there be? The vehicle is armored.

Getting into character, I hold out my arm for Mariana to take. Like a good actress who hates her costar, she places her hand softly on my forearm as if we were the closest of companions. We walk through the front door of the consulate, a striking couple. I secretly wish we really were a couple. But I know my past sins have forever condemned me in her eyes. Our appearance now is merely a well-planned charade and a prelude to the murder of a nation's corrupt and murderous leader.

We continue into a grand foyer lined with marble walls and exotic silk tapestries, probably Persian. I never would have guessed from the exterior that the interior would be so impressive. The furniture consists of contemporary polished metal and fine Italian leather, while the artwork is a blend of traditional paintings from the Afro-inspired northeastern Bahia area of Brazil and the ultramodern capital city of Brasilia. Positioned in the center of all these interesting paintings is an oversized portrait of Don Pedro himself. Like a bad movie villain, Don Pedro is portrayed in a white military uniform, adorned with an abundance of colorful medals, and a red sash that reads, "El Presidente." I couldn't make this up if I tried.

I look at Mariana and sarcastically remark, "El Presidente? Seriously?"

She just shakes her head. At least we both agree that Don Pedro is a buffoon.

A young waiter in a slim-fitting tuxedo approaches with a tray of champagne. We each take a glass and in an attempt to make Mariana relax a bit, I make a toast.

"To an enchanted evening."

"You really try hard, don't you?" she responds.

"What do you mean?" I ask.

"You must have had a lot of empty relationships with women."

"As a matter of fact, Mariana, I have. And if you read my file, you'll know why. You weren't the only one to lose a spouse."

At that moment, a short man with a beard interrupts our conversation with a boisterous declaration.

"Mariana, my dear, it is so wonderful to see you here!"

It is Consul General Rodrigo Hernandez.

"Rodrigo, you lovely man," she replies, "I wouldn't miss your parties for the world."

It's immediately obvious that Rodrigo is a dirty old man, probably in his late sixties, who wants to fuck Mariana.

*Get in line, pal.*

"And who is this? Your driver?" Hernandez smugly asks, as he looks me up and down.

"Oh, Rodrigo," Mariana covers for me, "I insist that you and the president meet with this gentleman. His name is Mr. Ward."

It's a pleasure to meet you, Mr. Hernandez," I say, extending my hand to him.

"*Buenas noches,*" he dryly replies in his native Spanish.

"Please forgive my attire. I just landed a few hours ago, and the airline lost my luggage. I had to purchase a suit on the way over here and this was the only thing I could find on such short notice. I assure you that when I am invited to meet with a man of your stature, I come appropriately dressed. I think that tonight there is a baggage handler in Campinas enjoying my Brioni suits."

Hernandez says nothing for what feels like forever then breaks out in laughter that grabs the attention of everyone at the party.

"I am sorry for your loss, Mr. Ward, but that is a hilarious story. I hope you find your luggage soon."

With that, Hernandez puts his arm around Mariana's waist and begins to walk her away from me. Realizing that my window of opportunity to make a first impression is closing quickly, I throw out one last line.

"I also find it hilarious, Mr. Hernandez, and oddly ironic. Suits were not the only items in my luggage. I also had an important gift in there for your brother, El Presidente."

Hernandez stops suddenly and turns back to look at me, still holding Mariana's waist.

"Really? What might that have been?"

I walk up close to him and whisper in his ear, "A very special pen."

Hernandez leans back from me. "A pen?"

"Not just any pen," I say in a low voice, careful not to let anyone but Mariana overhear. "But a magical pen that allows your brother to sign his name, just one time, and in return he will be rewarded with an abundance of cash, cheap oil for his country's citizens, and, most important, acceptance from the OAS, the United Nations, and even the US government. I guarantee this pen will make your brother's "President for Life" declaration completely legitimate in the eyes of the international community. But again, it's in my lost luggage. However, I'm sure that a man of your stature could help me find it. In return, I would be very grateful. And of course, so would El Presidente."

Hernandez stands quietly before me, never breaking eye contact. He is pondering what I just said. Either he is considering my offer or he is going to have security toss me out. After a few seconds, he drops his hand from around Mariana's waist and steps closer to me. With that same hand, he reaches up and places his palm on my shoulder.

"Señor Ward, is it? I think you and I should have a talk about your lost luggage in my office. I really want to help you find that pen."

"That would be fine. Thank you, Mr. Hernandez."

"Please call me Rodrigo."

He leads me across the foyer toward two large mahogany doors. Turning one of the polished brass doorknobs, he opens one of the doors and invites me to go in. Mariana trails two steps behind us. As Hernandez moves through the door, he turns back to face Mariana.

"I'm sorry, my dear, but Señor Ward and I must man-talk right now. I am sure you understand. Please don't go anywhere. I want to dance with you later."

With that, he closes the door on my partner's face. For the next forty-five minutes, I lay out a strategic overview for El Presidente's half-brother. I explain how my contacts will facilitate the transfer of oil via cargo ships from Brazil to other end-user countries but will make unscheduled refueling stops at one of his country's seaports. Then, some of the oil—which will not have been accounted for beforehand—will be secretly offloaded for Don Pedro's private use. He can sell it for profit, to buyers I can provide, or he can supplement the fuel used by his people.

I continue, explaining how I can help forge cargo manifests and circumvent customs inspections. Fortunately, Hernandez is not the smartest of men, and I find I can confuse him with an abundance of bullshit consulting jargon. I can tell he doesn't understand but is too proud to say so. This assures me he will recommend that I explain the plan to Don Pedro in person.

After ninety minutes, Hernandez and I emerge from his office laughing and smoking Partagas Robustos, fine Cuban cigars. The man has good taste in tobacco. Mariana is slumped at the bar alone stirring a Caipiroska. When she sees us, she snaps back into character and hurries across the room to give Hernandez a hug.

"Rodrigo, you two were in there forever. I was about to give up on your offer to dance with me."

"Ah, my darling Mariana. I was having a wonderful talk with my new friend here. I think I helped Paul find his lost luggage."

"That's wonderful, Rodrigo. I am so glad you two hit it off. I knew you would. Now how about that dance?"

"My sweet Mariana, I so want to dance with you right now, but alas my duty as Consul General calls. I must phone El Presidente right away about Paul's generous offer to consult for us. Hopefully, you will not hold this against me. May I take you to dinner tomorrow night to make it up to you? I promise, we shall dance the night away afterwards."

"I am busy tomorrow, Rodrigo," she demurs. "But I will take you up on your dinner invitation very soon. That is my promise."

Rodrigo turns to me and says, "Paul, it was a pleasure. I will be in touch."

"Thank you, Rodrigo, I look forward to speaking with El Presidente about his consulting needs."

With that, he disappears back into his office, a trail of cigar smoke floating in his wake.

"Sounds like you guys are new BFFs," Mariana jokes. "Before you know it you're going to start going on gay cruises together."

"Let's just hope he arranges this meeting with his brother soon so I don't have to work with you people anymore."

"I'm sorry about what I said earlier about your relationships. I didn't know you have lost people in your life, too."

"It's fine. At the end of the day, you're still a good person trying to do the right thing for your country, and I'm still some shitbag consultant."

"Right now, I don't know how righteous I can be. I am trying to assassinate someone, after all, with that same shitbag consultant—not to mention pretend to be attracted to that idiot Hernandez."

"Would you like to dance?" I ask, trying to change the subject.

"Don't you think Rodrigo would get jealous?" she replies, sounding a bit startled by my question.

"Fuck him. We're gonna poison his half-brother, anyway,

which probably means he'll eventually get taken out himself. Being jealous is the least of his concerns."

"In that case, I'm all yours tonight. I hope you're good on your feet!"

"I'm better on my back."

"I'll ignore that."

"Yeah, but I'll bet you dig it."

"Sadly, I think I'm starting to. I really need to get out of this business."

I extend my arm out to her again and lead Mariana to the dance floor. The live band begins to play Gilberto Gil's timeless hit "Aquele Abraço" (That Embrace). I put my left hand around Mariana's waist and take her hand with my right. Her back is more toned than I had imagined, and my chest brushes up against her firm breasts. They're so perfect that for a second I wonder if they're fake. I try to maintain eye contact with her and avoid staring at her cleavage. I can't believe this is the same woman who said that she was going to shoot me in the head earlier in the evening. I realize this is the reason I love Latin women: their extreme swings of passion.

We begin to samba seductively. Like most true Brazilian women, she is instinctively talented on the dance floor. I have to focus to keep up with her amazing rhythm. But the pleasure is all mine. For the first time, I see her smile.

The song ends, and the crowd applauds. The band changes its tune and begins playing a slower, even more seductive number, Antonio Carlos Jobim's romantic classic, "Wave." I wonder if it's appropriate to dance to a slow song with her, but Mariana seems fine with it. Therefore, so am I. We are now dancing with our faces just inches apart. She smells as incredible as she looks. I study her perfect face and think about the reality of embracing such a gorgeous woman.

"You know," I begin, "sometimes I forget what it was like back when I was a normal person. It's funny how one or two decisions can send your life down a totally different path."

"I know exactly what you mean," she agrees, looking into my eyes.

"If I had never run into my future mentor at a party," I continue, "the person who got me involved in this crazy line of work, I would probably be coaching high school football in the Midwest, driving a used Acura, and taking my wife and kids to Disney World every summer—kind of like Clark Griswold in *Vacation*."

She looks puzzled for a moment, and I realize that such an exotic creature has probably never heard of that silly movie. "No you wouldn't," she says. "You don't choose this life; it chooses you."

"You're saying it's fate that you and I are here dancing together right now?"

"Maybe it is," she says, smiling.

"In that case, I'm very grateful with the gods of fate for designing this moment."

"They didn't allow it. I did."

"That's good, because I think I would have more fun worshiping you than some pagan gods."

"Let's go home, Mr. Ward." Mariana says in a sexy voice.

"Absolutely," I respond.

With my arm around her, we quickly head out towards the front door. From the corner of my eye, I can see Rodrigo casting a disapproving look.

# THE MORNING AFTER

*Location:* Emiliano Hotel
*Time:* 0907 hours

I wake up in my king-sized bed with the light of the morning sun attempting to pry open my eyelids. *Damn sunlight! I should have invested in one of those ridiculous sleep masks that frequent fliers wear.* Despite my irritation, I open my eyes to the blinding white light of the São Paulo sunshine.

I am alone, feeling relaxed to the point of laziness—and am completely naked. My lack of clothing quickly reminds me of what an unforgettable night I just had. Mariana had driven me back to my hotel after we left the consulate and accepted my invitation to come up to my room for a drink—one reason why I always insist that my room has a stocked minibar.

Before we had even made it completely through the hotel room door, Mariana had me pushed up against the doorframe and began kissing my mouth hard—in that special way Brazilian girls are known for. I've always loved it when the woman takes the initiative. Then I took charge and tossed her down on the bed, after which we engaged in a competition to see who could undress the other first. We were both naked in record time and proceeded to make love like animals, void of romance and acting on purely carnal instinct. That was how we both wanted it, and neither of us said much. Our selfish intimacy seemed to go on repeatedly until we both feel asleep, exhausted at some unknown point during the early morning hours. Now, after that amazing experience, I find myself alone once more.

As I replay the highlights of the evening over and over in my head, I see something on the nightstand. It's a note from Mariana, written on hotel stationary and in her decidedly feminine hand. It reads: *Last night was a mistake. Forget it ever happened. Let's just finish the job. The next time I see you will be at the airport. M*

Suddenly I feel like a silly schoolboy who's been betrayed by his girlfriend for the first time. It's a complete role-reversal for me. I'm usually the one who leaves a note. Come to think of it, I usually just leave. But at the moment, I'm the one feeling used. I've never known what it feels like.

I hear a knock at the door and walk naked from the bed and look through the peephole. *Shit!* It's Joe. I run to the bathroom, wrap myself in a towel, and return to the door, opening it reluctantly.

"Rise and shine, dickhead," he says.

"Could you come back in an hour and bring me some fresh towels and an extra roll of toilet paper?" I respond sarcastically.

"Cut the jokes. I need a full debriefing on everything that happened last night," he barges past me into the room.

Joe seems all business this morning. He looks at the rolled up comforter on the bed and then scans the room as if he's searching for something—or someone. I decide to play dumb and avoid giving him any details.

"Didn't Mariana give you a report after we left the consulate?" I ask.

"I'm interested in your report right now," he snaps.

"Sure," I say. "It was very productive meeting, and Rodrigo has agreed to set a dinner with us and Don Pedro at El Presidente's private estate, just outside the capital, in three days. Everything's going exactly to plan."

"I understand you had a private conversation with Rodrigo."

"I did. He wouldn't let Mariana into the room with us. What could I do?"

"Don't fuck with me, Ward," he snaps. Joe has never called me by my last name before. It's apparent I shouldn't test him right now.

"I'm not," I respond respectfully.

*Shit!* I suddenly notice Mariana's note on the nightstand. I move around the bed and block Sparty's view of it. I reach down and pick up the telephone. As I do, I discreetly grab the note. Turning back around, I say, "I was gonna order some coffee. You want some?"

"Watch your ass and don't try any games with me. You're not off the hook yet. I can still put you in a deep hole that makes Gitmo look like a fuckin' Sandals Resort!"

I just nod. I feel silly standing there still in my towel holding the telephone receiver in one hand and Mariana's note behind me with the other.

"Jesus Christ!" Sparty says, shaking his head in disgust. "I still can't believe the boys in DC think this shitty plan is gonna work. It's the Fidel Castro debacle all over again." A reference to the CIA's repeated failed assassination attempts against the Cuban dictator back in the '60s.

Joe's snarkiness seems to have cranked up a notch. I'm guessing he's pissed that I left with Mariana last night and suspects that I got what he's been craving.

"Go buy yourself some new clothes and await further instructions. You and Mariana will take a private jet from Guarulhos in three days, and we'll need to use all the time between now and then to prep for the operation. Stay close to the cell phone I gave you."

"You got it," I say like a good soldier.

Joe looks at me one more time suspiciously—as if he does not trust me, which of course he does not—and heads toward the door. Before stepping out, he gives me one final piece of advice.

"Oh, if you have any thoughts of trying to slip away to some other country instead of living up to your end of the bargain, just know that there's a highly specialized surveillance team watching your every move. You do anything out of the ordinary and it would be my pleasure to cancel this fucked-up operation and have you hanged for treason."

As he slams the door behind him, I consider the thought of being public enemy number one. It is sobering.

Is there really a surveillance team? If so, then Joe must know about Mariana and me. In fact, wouldn't there be cameras in the room, as well? Too many thoughts are now racing through my head too early in the morning. I decide to order some breakfast to help me focus. I call room service and request two eggs over easy, *pão na chapa* (traditional Brazilian bread grilled with butter), fresh-squeezed orange juice, and a triple espresso. As I hang up the phone, there is another knock at the door. *What now?*

I open the door to see a five-foot-two Chinese man. He has a big smile on his face and is wearing a light-blue seersucker suit with a white Panama hat. He carries a garment bag over his shoulder.

"Hey, Mr. Mister. Long time, no see!"

"Bruce W. Lee, my man!"

Still standing in my towel, I give the little man a bro' hug in the doorway.

"Get your Chairman Mao-looking ass in here!" I instruct him.

Bruce W. Lee has been my go-to guy for logistical support for years in Brazil. It's absolutely amazing what this little turd can acquire: anything from guns, to drugs, to girls. Even radioactive material, Mr. Lee can get it for you. He was named after the martial arts legend Bruce Lee, though he's much more dangerous with his Rolodex, not his fists. Also, he will never admit to anyone what his middle initial *W* stands for. He usually tells everyone to just call him "BW," which he likes to claim that the ladies say stands for "Big Wang." I have always called him Mr. Lee and he—because I have never given him my name—just calls me Mr. Mister.

In addition to Portuguese, Chinese, and broken English, Mr. Lee speaks flawless Arabic and Farsi. This makes him a regular buyer and seller in the vaunted Tri-Border Area, South America's equivalent to Afghanistan's FATA, the no-man's land where illegal goods—anything from weapons to knock-off hand bags—are manufactured and traded between the borders of Brazil, Argentina and Paraguay.

Don't let his small size and large smile fool you; Mr. Lee is a very dangerous and deals with some of the world's most heinous scoundrels. Maybe it should concern me that we get along so well.

"Lee, I need a favor," I begin. "But first, I have a feeling the room might be bugged."

"Ha! Not to worry," he tells me reaching into his jacket.

He pulls out a black device that resembles a 1980s cell phone, the kind Gordon Gekko used in the movie *Wall Street*.

With a big smile, he continues. "This jam all audio and video frequencies. Even your television no work with this thing running. Go on, try it."

I grab the television remote and hit the power button. Nothing but static appears on every channel. I then notice that the numbers on the digital alarm clock have begun blinking frantically. Mr. Lee strikes again.

"Lee, you're a genius. But I also think there's a team that's conducting physical surveillance on me at the moment, too."

"Not to worry," he assures me again. "When I got your signal to meet, I assumed you want our traditional cover story. Therefore, I tell people at front desk I your tailor and that you request me to measure you for suits. I bring couple of Brionis in your size here in garment bag. Some shoes, too."

"Good man!"

"Okay, tell me what I can do for you this time."

"I have someone I need you to follow so I can figure out if I'm being set up."

"No problem. Hopefully, she pretty," he jokes.

"Don't worry, she is."

"Need usual stuff?"

"Yes, and I need it within forty-eight hours. But there's something else. I don't have access to my bank account right now. So I'm gonna pay you double as soon as I can break free from this surveillance team."

"No problem, Mr. Mister. Your credit always good with me. I come back in forty-eight hours with new suits and the information you need."

"You're the best, Lee. So, now will you tell me what the hell the *W* stands for?"

He breaks out in a big smile and says, "When you tell me your real name."

"I guess it's gonna be a long time, then."

Yet another knock on the door. My breakfast has arrived but I suspect it's one of the surveillance team members trying to figure out why they lost audio and video reception. Lee quickly unzips the garment bag and throws a few suits on the bed. He then wraps a measuring tape around his neck, as if he has been measuring my inseam, which would be kind of awkward since I'm still in my towel. I open the door to see what appears to be a hotel employee replete in white, button-down shirt and black vest, and with a nametag that reads, *Carlos*.

For a guy pushing a room-service cart he seems awfully fit. I estimate he could bench press at least 300 pounds. I notice a tattoo on his wrist: a sword and shield. I decide to give him a tip of fifty reais (about fifteen dollars) just to gauge his reaction. He takes the money like a robot, says "*obrigado*," and then departs.

Lee looks at me and says, "You give him 50 reais and he not even smile. He definitely surveillance team."

*This isn't good,* I think to myself.

"Lee, I really need you to deliver on this one. Otherwise, you might see me on CNN someday hanging by my neck on the front lawn of the White House."

Lee laughs and tells me, "Mr. Mister, I don't know who you really are, but you have one crazy job!"

# COLD SHOULDER

**Location:** *Aboard a Private Jet*
**Time:** *1230 hours*

Mariana and I are sitting in uncomfortable silence as our Gulfstream IV silently races above the Amazon rainforest at 600 miles per hour. Since meeting at the airport less than four hours ago, we have not really spoken much, other than trading a couple of "*bom dias*" on the tarmac. She has been busy pretending to be reading the contents of a government manila folder, and I have remained thoroughly engaged with stirring my Old Fashioned on the rocks. At least the plush Italian leather swivel chair I'm sitting in is amazingly comfortable.

The dark-skinned stewardess with the thick *carioca* accent who prepared my drink, despite putting in too many drops of bitters, is wearing the tightest black pants, which perfectly accentuate her lovely Brazilian butt. *What is it with Latin women and tight black pants?* In order to not upset Mariana, I attempt to conceal my ogling. I then try to gauge which one of them has a better rear end, Mariana or this stewardess? Actually, it's no contest. The stewardess is undeniably attractive, but Mariana is legendary. I'm discouraged over the idea that I may never see her naked again. It's time for me to break the ice.

"Mariana, may I tell you how incredible you look today?"

"Tell it to the stewardess. You've been removing her slacks with your eyes since we boarded." Ouch!

"Actually, I've been undressing both of you, and you can't believe what else I have you two doing."

"You want her? Go get her," she says, without even looking up from her papers.

"Do I detect a hint of jealousy?" I say, trying to sound playful.

Now she looks up and checks to see if the stewardess is out of earshot.

"You need to understand something, Mr. Ward."

*Really? She just called me Mr. Ward?*

"We're on our way to conduct a very important operation, one that is going to change a country's history—one that could get us both killed. You need to take this seriously."

"First of all," I shoot back, "my name is Paul. Or, if you prefer, you can call me '*gostoso*' (Portuguese for tasty). Next, I'm always serious about my work. How the hell do you think I've been able to operate right under the noses of every intelligence service and law-enforcement agency across the globe for the past twenty years? And lastly, I'm a professional consultant, not a hit man, which makes this ridiculous plan of yours all the more fucked up. I mean, come on, you send a team of Navy SEALs into Pakistan to kill Osama bin Laden, but you're sending me to off this dictator? The whole thing makes zero sense. If anyone needs to get serious, it's you guys."

"You have no idea what it takes to preserve democracy," she snaps.

"Preserve democracy? That's your justification? Who the hell is pulling your strings, lady?"

"This isn't up for debate—*Paul*. Remember, just do the job and you walk. Don't do the job and spend the rest of your life in prison—or worse. End of discussion."

"Fine!" I bark.

"Yes, fine!" she counters.

The stewardess hears us and emerges from the galley.

"*Dá licença, que a gente tá conversando aqui. . . vaca!*" Mariana yells. "*Pode voltar pra copa!*" The unsuspecting stewardess retreats in stunned silence.

"Jesus, was that really necessary?"

She slams the manila folder on her tray in front of her.

"I'm sorry," she says in a quivering voice, "You're right, this plan doesn't make any sense at all. I can't believe I agreed to this shit."

Her eyes tear up, ever so slightly.

"I should apologize to that girl," she says remorsefully, and rises to walk toward the galley.

"Hey," I say in a soft voice.

"Yes?" She stops, turns and looks tenderly at me for the first time today.

"Tell her to bring me another Old Fashioned, but go easy on the bitters this time."

Mariana frowns at me with a look that says, "You're an asshole."

You might think I'm being unfair to Mariana, and I probably am. But there's a good reason for it. When Mr. Lee returned to my hotel room after forty-eight hours, as he promised, he once again used his cover as my tailor to bring me my new suits and, more importantly, new information. Mr. Lee had put Mariana under surveillance and hacked into her personal emails. Not an easy task, with Mariana being a trained intelligence officer who's accustomed to detecting surveillance and practicing good OPSEC—operational security.

But Mariana has never met the likes of someone as devious as Lee. When he discovered that she jogged near her apartment every morning at around six-thirty, and always ran along the same route while listening to her iPod shuffle, he devised a simple plan. Lee assumed that Mariana was too smart to fall for the old trick of simply clicking on a dummy email, which would allow a hacker to gain access to her computer. He also assumed she maintained updated antivirus software.

Not to worry, as he says. He quickly found another way into her email inbox.

Before one of her morning jogs, Lee left a bright-blue iPod Shuffle on the sidewalk along her chosen path. The idea was that another runner had accidently dropped the iPod and kept on running. When Mariana spotted the device, she picked it up—while Lee watched from the bushes to confirm the pickup. She then dutifully asked all the other runners she came across if they had lost it, but no one claimed it. So Mariana took the iPod home and plugged it into her laptop to see if there was any evidence of its owner.

To Mariana's surprise, the iPod was filled with close to one hundred hit songs, in both English and Portuguese. Impressed by the playlist, Mariana began dragging some of the songs from the iPod onto to her computer's playlist. As she transferred the files, she also unknowingly allowed Mr. Lee's virus to infect her email inbox. As a result, Mr. Lee gained access to all of Mariana's personal emails, which he then printed out and brought to me at my hotel room, concealed in the garment bag with the Brioni suits.

The content of those emails made me rethink the entire operation.

Mariana returns from the jet's galley and walks toward me. She has apparently apologized to the stewardess, given the relieved look on her face. She is also carrying my fresh drink.

"Everything okay?" I ask.

"Yes, everything is okay. I apologized to the girl and told her I was upset because you were staring at her ass. She apparently seemed flattered by that and then asked if you and I were a couple."

"What did you say?"

"I said, yes, we are, and invited her for a threesome tonight."

"Really?" I ask, suddenly intrigued.

"No, dumbass. I told her that you were some loser pervert, and now she's too scared to even come back out here again."

"Thanks a lot."

"It's better this way. Now we have complete privacy," she says in a seductive voice, straddling my legs while handing me my drink.

"Wait a minute. Two minutes ago you hated me. Now you're sitting on my lap? Why the sudden change of heart?"

"Doesn't a woman have the right to change her mind? Besides, I just realized that whether this operation is total success of a complete failure, I'm probably never going to see you again. So, I might as well enjoy myself."

She starts to unbutton my shirt. After an hour or so of enjoying each other's company on the leather sofa in the jet's cabin, Mariana has returned to her seat, once again reading through her government folder. It's apparent to me she was nervous about the operation and needed a way to release some stress. I, of course, was happy to oblige. What is it about private jets that turn women on so much?

I'm in no way complaining about my current situation. I recognize when I'm being played for a fool. Mariana still doesn't know I've read her personal emails and understand the full scope of her plans for me. I also know her other secret—that she and Joe are in a relationship.

# GOLDEN GOOSE

**Location:** *El Presidente's VVIP Terminal*
**Time:** *1605 hours*

The Gulfstream's wheels gently touch down on the runway as we arrive in Don Pedro's homeland. Outside the windows is a lush, tropical landscape filled with bright colors set against a stunning, mountainous backdrop. Steam is rising off the plant life, a result of a recent rainstorm. It's hard to believe this jungle paradise is in such disarray. Why can't Disney run Latin America, instead of corrupt dictators and politicians?

It has always bothered me that these countries are so full of natural resources yet maintain such poor infrastructure, high unemployment, and low wages, and are unnecessarily reliant on loans from the International Monetary Fund. I would be willing to bet that if you brought in a local city council from any small town in Nebraska, those ethical, God-fearing patriots who believe in earning your keep and maintaining a smart fiscal budget, you could improve the management of most Latin American countries tenfold.

Forget calling in a bunch of Harvard MBAs from consulting firms such as McKinsey or Bain. Just clean out all the *jefes* in power and replace them with people with common sense. Then perhaps Latin America would become the economic powerhouse it should be. Maybe that's what my current employers are intending to do.

As the jet rolls to a stop, Mariana and I get up and walk to the front of plane. As we do, the sexy stewardess, who has remained tucked away in her galley, shoots me a look of disdain. I haven't seen her since Mariana told her to give us privacy. Her scowl makes me think Mariana told her something pretty awful about me. That, coupled with the fact that she probably snuck a peek at Mariana and me fooling around on the back couch, must make her dislike me even more.

But then, I'm not here to make friends but to kill a president.

The jet's door opens and the staircase unfolds. I let Mariana go first and step out into a wave of humidity comparable to a steam room. We immediately begin sweating through our shirts, and beads of perspiration erupt on our foreheads. I am dehydrated, and immediately regret drinking those glasses of bourbon on the flight.

A black Mercedes slowly pulls up on the tarmac and stops a few feet from us. A young man in his early twenties, wearing a white chauffeur's uniform, pops out and hurries around to open the rear door facing us. Our good buddy Rodrigo from the São Paulo consulate emerges with a smile.

"Ah, Mariana my love, how are you? You look more beautiful than ever!"

"I'm wonderful, Rodrigo. It's so nice to see you here. What a pleasant surprise."

Mariana's response is in her best actress voice.

Rodrigo turns to me and says, "And Señor Ward, it is great to see you, my friend. Welcome to our humble country."

"Thank you, Rodrigo. It is a pleasure to be here," I lie.

The three of us get into the Mercedes. Mariana and Rodrigo sit in the back and I sit in the front. I can't help but notice that Rodrigo has placed his hand on Mariana's knee. She allows him to do so—it's part of the job. How is it that Mariana can go through life using her female powers of persuasion to accomplish her goals? I find it sad. But who am I to make moral judgments?

"El Presidente is incredibly busy these days. Therefore we are going to see him right away while his schedule has an opening," Rodrigo informs us.

"All the better," Mariana responds.

We drive from the VVIP (Very Very Important Person)

terminal at the airport out onto the highway. As we navigate the potholed road, we can see shantytowns on both sides. Once again, I think there is no reason for all this poverty.

"As you can see, Señor Ward, we have many poor people in our country. That is why we need your help to find increased streams of revenue to lift them out of misery."

"That's what I'm here for," I dryly reply, now looking out the windshield.

After forty minutes of what seems like aimless driving through the countryside, we approach the decadent presidential mansion of Don Pedro. Its strange design is part antebellum Southern plantation, part medieval castle, and part Mediterranean villa. I'm not really sure what the architect was going for. The only thing that seems to pull the structure together is its coat of bright white paint, which is accentuated even more against the tropical foliage.

The Mercedes pulls up the driveway as numerous guards, lining the pavement in their military fatigues, snap to attention. We come to a stop and disembark toward the ornate front door complemented with a golden lion's head to intimidate visitors. As we walk up the few marble steps onto the front porch, the lion's head retracts inward when the front door opens. Then the man himself, El Presidente, emerges in its place. He is wearing a popular white *guayabera* dress shirt, with tan linen pants and woven leather shoes. What few hairs he has on his head are slicked back and dyed a jet-black color to match his bushy mustache. A cigar juts out of his breast pocket, and his accessories include a diamond encrusted gold Rolex, thick gold chain with a crucifix pendant, and set of gaudy rings—complete with turquoise and emerald stones—that would have made Liberace jealous. He is every bad stereotype of a South American dictator personified. The best way to describe him is as a cross between former Brazilian President Luiz Inácio Lula da Silva, whom the North America media deemed "Brazil's outgoing and lovable buffoon," and a bad druglord from an old episode of the '80s TV show *Miami Vice*.

"*Bienvenidos*, my friends!" he proclaims, walking toward us with arms opened wide. He of course makes a beeline for Mariana. Wrapping his arms around her, he squeezes her close then kisses her on the cheek, delivering a line that would make even Bill Clinton cringe.

"Child, your beauty could make the Virgin Mary cry!"

Mariana smiles and drops her head like an embarrassed schoolgirl, while I try to figure out what the fuck he means—or if Mariana even knows.

Don Pedro, still grasping Mariana's waist with both hands, turns to me next and says, "Señor Ward, I am pleased to meet you and welcome you as my guest."

"Señor, it is an honor to be in your presence, particularly here at your lovely home," I reply dutifully.

"Thank you, but it is the people's home, Señor Ward. I am merely a humble servant to their wishes for a better life. They have given me the honored privilege to serve them and represent their best interests."

What a crock of shit! This guy has designed, built, and lived in the "people's home" for over a decade. Despite what the people really want. And Don Pedro has no intention of turning over the keys to the castle anytime soon.

That said, I give him a few points for the bullshit line, though he probably picked that one up from one of his fellow leaders.

I attempt to outdo him at creating a steaming pile of bullshit.

"You are a man of great humility, El Presidente. I admire your selflessness in putting your fellow countrymen first. That is rare trait found only in the greatest leaders throughout history."

He apparently appreciates the compliment and invites us inside. As we walk through the lion-headed front door, his arm remains around Mariana's waist. I have to smile at the irony of it all. Here I am, an American capitalist welcomed by a corrupt socialist dictator—Latin American politics at its finest.

After a brief tour of the ostentatious mansion, whose interior is loosely designed after the Palais Versailles, we are led into the presidential dining room for lunch. It is all formality: 22-karat gold utensils, flowers in vintage crystal vases, white-gloved wait staff, and an impressive seating arrangement where each of our names is etched into a small rectangular glass block in front of our place setting. A polished sommelier, dressed in a navy-blue Tom Ford suit that must have cost $7,500, pours a $500 bottle of Opus One red into each of our glasses.

Yes, Don Pedro would be a golden goose of a client to any consultant of my ilk.

Don Pedro, now seated at the head of the long table, which could easily accommodate twenty guests, raises his glass in what can either be considered a toast or a prayer.

"My friends, may we give thanks to God for the opportunity of all of us gathering here today. Every meal shared with guests is a blessing that should not be discounted. May this bountiful lunch enrich us to make wise decisions, in order to benefit the people of this great nation."

"Hear, hear!" Rodrigo approves.

"Hear, hear," Mariana and I respond.

Don Pedro turns and nods to an older gentleman with slicked white hair, wearing a black and white tuxedo, who is standing attentively near the wall. This man is obviously the headwaiter. The other servers are wearing white dinner jacket tuxedos. The headwaiter claps his hands rapidly, and his minions scurry like trained mice to serve the food. We begin with a Waldorf salad, which could rival the original version served in New York City, followed by our appetizers: shrimp *rojo y verde*. Amazing.

After a small martini glass of mint sorbet to cleanse our palates, our main course arrives: filet mignon in red wine sauce with truffle butter and a side of white asparagus.

I mentally tip my hat to Don Pedro. For a man born into poverty who climbed his way up the greasy rungs of his society's ladder, via political posturing and literal backstabbing, he has evolved into a man with impeccable taste in food.

Don Pedro reminds me of dictators such as a Saddam Hussein or Muammar Gaddafi, who, despite their outward cruelty and murderous reigns, wielded a positive controlling effect over their chaos-infected societies. There is even an international consulting term for this phenomenon. It's called the *Under the Thumb Rule*. It states it's easier to control the masses through fear and repression than with freedom of speech and democratically elected governments. Guys like me make our money by suggesting ways dictators, such as Don Pedro, can increase wealth and power. He is the golden goose and I'm here to catch some eggs.

"Don Pedro, you have graciously agreed to meet with me

and allow me to share my ideas on how best to stimulate your country's economy. Perhaps now is a good time for me to offer my insights and suggestions?"

"By all means, Señor Ward."

"Thank you, El Presidente. As you well know, moving oil through the region is a lucrative business. So much so that oil-producing countries are reaping the benefits of the industry and using their newly found wealth to allow many of their lower-class citizens to move into the middle class. This has improved the purchasing power of millions, which in turn stimulates the economies of those countries and places them on a more solid footing on the international stage. This in turn leads to increased investment from outsiders, increased revenues from tourism, a stronger currency, improved infrastructure, and enhanced education. In short, the oil producers are becoming richer nations, while the non-producing nations are being left behind."

"Tell us something we don't already know, Señor Ward," says an unimpressed Don Pedro.

"Well, sir, the way I see it, the only real non-oil producing country that seems to be benefiting from this phenomenon is Panama. Because of the canal, they can act as a hub for shipping, and thus Panama is the only country collecting massive taxes and enjoying a cash surplus."

"Again, señor, this is all common knowledge," says Don Pedro.

"Yes, El Presidente. But what if you could steal some of that business away from Panama?"

"Go on."

"I have connections within a neighbor country's government that are ready to divert shipping and refueling activities to your country—for a moderate fee, of course."

"Of course," he affirms.

"The tradeoff would consist of unaccountable oil in return for lower dockage and refueling fees, not to mention a few mutually beneficial agreements pertaining to OAS and U.N. votes. Not only would your economy improve from the increased maritime traffic, but you would also have enough excess oil—hundreds of millions of dollars' worth, which of course would be off the books—to use at your discretion. It is the ultimate win-win scenario."

Don Pedro looks at me skeptically, while Mariana and Rodrigo appear to be hanging anxiously on his reply.

After a few seconds, which feel more like minutes, Don Pedro casually takes a sip of his wine, wipes his lips, and then clears his throat to speak.

"Señor Ward, I thank you for your suggestion. You are a very smart man. Perhaps too smart. Now, allow me to give you my thoughts in rebuttal."

Everyone at the table is quiet, as Don Pedro once again exercises a dramatic pause.

"I grew up in a tiny village twenty miles from this amazing presidential mansion—here, where we have just enjoyed this lavish capitalist lunch. When I was a boy, such a meal would have fed my entire family for a month. Did you know that I did not wear my first pair of shoes until I was thirteen years old? Yet, despite my simple upbringing, I have risen to the highest position of power in my modest country. How do you think I accomplished this?"

"Persistence," is all I can respond.

"Ha! Persistence is just one of my virtues, Señor Ward. But I achieved my success by following my instincts, which were honed on the streets, and by surrounding myself only with people with whom I can entrust my life. People like Rodrigo, my half-brother here."

"That is a wise philosophy," Mariana chimes in.

"Mariana, you silly girl. Do you not know I have been onto your connections with the US government for years? You allow Rodrigo to fondle your body while you attempt to elicit him for intelligence, in hopes that you can go back to your real handlers and get credit for the worthless cables you write up for their masters back at Langley? I did not become the leader of this nation without my own ability to collect intelligence, and I have a feeling that my sources are much more reliable than yours."

"Don Pedro," stumbles Mariana, "I have no idea what you are talking about. I am simply a consular officer at the US Embassy. I'm afraid your sources have painted me to be someone that I am not."

"Enough games, señora."

Don Pedro nods to Rodrigo, who springs from his seat, grabs Mariana's arms, and pins them behind her back.

"Let go of me!" she screams.

"I'm sorry, Mariana, but I have owed you this for a long time," Rodrigo says through his teeth.

"Paul, do something!" she implores me.

Don Pedro looks at her and grins in satisfaction.

"Señora, your friend Paul cannot help you. You see, Señor Ward has been in my employ for many years. In fact, we have a business relationship that goes back before you began working for your employer. I know all about your plot to assassinate me. I'm afraid your attempt to recruit him has been, shall we say, unsuccessful?"

Mariana's eyes open wide as she scowls at me.

"You bastard! Why? Why would you sell out your country for this worthless piece of shit?"

"It's simple, Mariana," I reply, "He pays better. Plus, I always know where I stand with a dictator. I can hardly say the same about the American imperialists!"

Mariana spits in my face before Rodrigo lifts her up from under her arms and drags her out of the room.

Don Pedro smiles at me and raises his wine glass. "To you, Paul, for being my most esteemed adviser."

I use my napkin to wipe the spit off my face.

# AMIGO

*Location:* Don Pedro's Presidential Balcony
*Time:* 1830 hours

It has been over an hour since Rodrigo, with assistance from a few of his security staff, dragged Mariana out of the dining room. She put up a good fight, but eventually the sounds of her shouting obscenities in Portuguese disappeared down the corridors.

As the well-trained wait staff clears the table of our delicious lunch, Don Pedro and I are each enjoying a *Romeo y Julieta* cigar, accompanied with a snifter of Ron del Barrilito—the finest rum known to man—while we stand on the marble balcony overlooking the mansion's expansive lawn. The manicured grass, trees, and plants remind me of a botanical garden. Exotic animals roam the grounds, like a zoo. It actually resembles Saddam Hussein's old palace in Baghdad. The setting is incredibly relaxed, and El Presidente and I are reminiscing about old times.

"So, *amigo*," Don Pedro begins, puffing on his cigar, "I am surprised it has been a few years since you and I enjoyed cigars like this."

"Too long," I agree, "I think the last time we did it was six years ago in Miami. Remember when we picked up those Puerto Rican girls at the Delano Hotel on South Beach? What a crazy night that was!"

"*Dios mio!* I forgot about that shit. I did so much cocaine off that *chica's culo* my head almost exploded. No wonder I stopped hanging out with you!"

"No," I remind him. "The reason we stopped hanging out was because you got too comfortable moving narcotics through your airport, and the DEA got pissed and limited your personal travel."

"I know, I know. Damned DEA! Another American agency that has no business in my country. Speaking of business, how is life in the global consulting game? I heard a rumor that Yuri fucked you over in Afghanistan."

"He did. But that's between him and me, and I have the situation under control."

"*Amigo*," he says, laughing. "I have known you for a long time. You are an excellent consultant, but a lousy tough guy. May you never have to serve time in a Latin American prison."

"What the hell does that mean?"

"It means you are consultant, not a hit man. I find it funny that the Americans would even consider you as an option to take me out. When Rodrigo informed me of the plan, after your private meeting with him in São Paulo, my first reaction was not one of concern but one of laughter. I mean, really, Marcus, you and I both know that your profession is built upon sand. You're a middle man, not a killer."

Yes, you heard right. Don Pedro knows me as *Marcus*.

"So are you saying that Yuri has nothing to worry about?" I ask in a serious tone.

"Oh, Marcus. I am saying that if you play with fire you could get burned. Yuri is Russian mafia. They are not exactly—how do you say—Boy Scouts."

"You don't know me as well as you think, Don Pedro," I counter.

"I am not challenging your manhood, *amigo*. You just need to understand you are out of your element. *Por ejemplo*."

Don Pedro reaches behind his back, pulls out a silver-plated Glock 17 9-millimeter handgun, and presents it to me.

"Do you know how to use one of these?"

"Of course," I say.

"Prove it."

"How?"

"You see that flock of birds about fifty meters away on the lawn?"

"You mean those exotic peacocks?"

"Yes, those exotic peacocks."

"I'm not going to shoot a fucking peacock!"

"Don't worry, *amigo*. I have so many of those damn birds you would be doing me a favor. They shit on everything. Go on, show me you have the accuracy of a killer."

I take the pistol and with my right arm hold it straight out in front of me. I close my left eye and line one of the peacocks up with the site post on the tip of the barrel. I gently squeeze the trigger. The gun recoils back in my wrist. I miss the colorful bird by a mile, and the annoying sound of squawking peacocks is now everywhere. Don Pedro is beside himself with laughter.

"That was embarrassing, *amigo*! You want to exact revenge against the Russian mob, but you cannot even kill a stupid bird from fifty meters!"

"Okay, Pedro. Why don't you show me how it's done?"

He suddenly stops laughing and stares at me in anger. Apparently he does not like to be called just Pedro. He sets his snifter of rum down on the thick marble ledge of the balcony and grabs the pistol out of my hand.

Leaning forward over the ledge, he lines up the shot. Using two hands on the weapon and standing with his feet apart, he rolls his shoulders forward a few times, as if to loosen up. He closes his left eye and begins to search out his victim. When he determines which bird it will be, he smiles.

As he readies for the kill, I ever so subtly move next to him on his left side—the side next to his closed eye. While he fixates on his target, I hover my left cufflink over his exposed glass. With my right hand I gently pop open the pearl cap, releasing the clear powder into his drink. The colorless and odorless poison is now in place.

There is a loud crack, as Don Pedro fires the 9mm handgun, which is immediately followed by dull thud.

"Ah ha!" he screams. "A direct hit!"

I look across the lawn and one of the majestic birds is lifeless on the ground. At least it didn't suffer.

"Fuck me, what a great shot!" I say, complimenting him.

"You see, *amigo*? That is how you kill. And believe me, it is much harder to kill a trained Russian mobster, who is shooting back at you, than some dumb animal."

"You took the words right out of my mouth," I concur.

"*Amigo,* let me give you some advice. You have made a lot of money over the years. Perhaps it is time you take that small fortune of yours, move to a nice island somewhere, and start a family. You are not getting any younger. Enjoy the rest of your life. Forget about Yuri and just retire already."

I look Don Pedro directly in the eyes and say, "I think you're right. As of now, I am officially retired."

I pick up my glass of rum and hold it up in a toast. Don Pedro reaches down next to him and grabs his snifter filled with the poison.

"To retirement!" I proclaim.

"To retirement!" he repeats.

We each take a long pull of our drinks.

Thank you, my friend," I say. "I am going to miss our little chats together."

Don Pedro smiles and throws his arm—the one still holding the pistol—around my neck. He speaks to me in a fatherly tone.

"Marcus, you saved my life. If you hadn't told Rodrigo about the US government's plan to assassinate me, I might already be dead. I owe you a debt of gratitude."

"What are friends for?" I respond.

"For your loyalty, *amigo,* I have made all of the necessary arrangements. I have wired ten million US dollars to your bank account in Switzerland; I have prepared for you a diplomatic passport from my country, and you are booked on the six o'clock flight to Miami tonight in first class. *Gracias por todo!*"

"*De nada,*" I respond. "*Y muchas gracias por todo.*"

# NOW YOU SEE ME . . .

**Location:** *Miami Beach*
**Time:** *0715 hours*

I am standing on the beach, running shoes and socks in hand, watching the sunrise. I woke up early and decided to go for a run along the sand to break a sweat and clear my head. Despite the time, the beach is already starting to fill up. It is mostly older couples, many New York snowbirds in ridiculous looking—and, worse, matching—track suits and oversized dark sunglasses, out for their morning walks. A heavy-set older Cuban man, wearing nothing but a black thong bathing suit, gaudy gold chain around his neck, walks past me sweeping a metal detector back-and-forth over the sand, looking for trinkets left behind by tourists. I gaze out over the Atlantic Ocean, as the sun begins its daily climb from below the horizon. In my iPod earphones, Phil Collins sings, *"I don't care anymore I don't care no more!"*

At that moment, I ask myself if I still care about anything—or anyone. It's been two weeks since I boarded Don Pedro's private jet and headed up to Miami. Normally, I would have immediately changed my identity and boarded another flight for Europe to put as much distance possible between myself from my last consulting engagement. But avoiding my better judgment this time, I've opted to hang out in South Beach.

My thoughts linger on Mariana. Where is she? Will she ever forgive me? Will Joe Sparty and his employers seek unmerciful revenge against me for exposing them and placing her in danger?

For the first time in a long time, I feel guilt. More than anything, that's probably why I've stayed in Miami. Maybe I want to be caught. Maybe it's time I stop running and face prison for all my global misconduct? It's difficult for me to form a clear thought right now.

I booked a suite at the Fontainebleau, the same hotel where James Bond first matched wits against his nemesis Auric Goldfinger in the third James Bond movie. Every night since, I have been eating and drinking too much and partying with a different Latina girl, each of which has been cosmetically enhanced and is nothing but trouble. I must have dropped at least fifty grand since I've been here. I have put my business, and my thoughts of retribution against Yuri, on indefinite hold. Right now, just like Phil Collins, I guess I don't care.

A loud annoying beeping noise snaps me back into reality.

"Aha!" yells the old man with the metal detector, which is now squawking even louder and quicker.

I look over to see him bent over, his fat ass sprouting from the thong staring back at me, digging something out of the sand. He stands up straight and holds before him what appears to be a gold wedding band.

"Success!" he declares triumphantly.

"Congratulations," I offer.

"*Gracias,*" he replies.

"Is it valuable?"

"Who cares?" he shrugs.

His response confuses me, so I decide to follow up.

"Why bother to waste your time coming out here if you don't care about the value of what you find?"

"My friend," smiles the old man, "as you get older, you realize that life is more about the search for something rather than the discovery. Hell, I've been out here every morning for the past two weeks and haven't found anything. I was about ready to throw this thing in the ocean. However, this silly piece of jewelry has just given me a shot of adrenaline and the will to keep searching again tomorrow. Life is good right now."

The old man is so proud of himself that all I can say back to him is, "Good hunting."

I start walking back to my hotel.

After a quick shower in my room, I throw on a pair of tan linen pants, a navy-blue polo, and Havaianas flip-flops. I head down to breakfast and take a seat at a small table near the hotel's massive swimming pool. My morning run has inspired me, and I decide it's time to start eating healthier again. A pretty young Hispanic waitress, whom I assume to be a college student, takes my order. I request an egg-white omelet, a bowl of granola with fruit, a tall orange juice, and a double espresso. Before she leaves, the waitress asks me if I'd like a newspaper. Being out of the media loop for the past few weeks, I simply reply with a nod to indicate yes.

A minute later, the girl returns with a copy of the Miami Herald. She sets it down in front of me, and the first thing I see is the bold headline, *Latin America Dictator Dies Suddenly— Foreign Minister Assumes Control of Country.*

I can feel the bump in my heart rate. So, it's done. The slow poison I discreetly dumped into Don Pedro's drink worked. I read deeper into the article, as beads of sweat form on my forehead:

*According to the statement put out by the president's office, the leader known as Don Pedro died of complications believed to be the result of pneumonia. He had taken power of the country twenty years ago as part of a bloody coup. Ever since, the country has suffered massive economic hardship, human rights violations, and corruption scandals. The Foreign Minister, his half-brother, Rodrigo Hernandez, was named successor on a temporary basis. No word on when or if elections will be held to confirm Mr. Hernandez's claim to the presidency.*

\* \* \*

Time to come clean. Back at the party at the consulate in São Paulo, I cut a secret deal with Rodrigo. I promised him that I could cleanly kill his brother, using the special poison provided by the Americans, so he could take control of the country unopposed. As part of the deal, Rodrigo would have to tell Don Pedro the USG was planning to kill him. This would free me from the agency, via the clean passport, private jet, and cash provided by El Presidente.

Once I secured those details, it was easy for me to get close enough to Don Pedro and administer the poison. The most important part of the plan was that Mariana could not know about the deal. Therefore, Rodrigo had to promise me that when he ratted out Mariana to Don Pedro, she would not be harmed and would be returned safely to Brazil as soon as he took power.

It was the only part of the plan that worried me. I still had no idea what had become of Mariana. For all I knew she could be sitting in a prison cell, or worse, being raped and tortured daily by prison guards.

\* \* \*

The waitress returns with my double espresso and orange juice. I tell her to cancel the rest of my order and bring me my check immediately. I've essentially come to my senses. I can't spend any more time in the United States. I slug down the coffee and juice, and twenty minutes later I've packed my suitcase and grab a taxi headed for Miami International Airport. I am checking flight schedules on my phone en route.

\* \* \*

A few hours have passed and I am now sitting in upper class on a Virgin Atlantic flight to London's Heathrow Airport. When I land, I will send Mariana an email from the business lounge, which I am drafting on my laptop at the moment. It reads:

Mariana,

By now you and your colleagues have figured out that Rodrigo and I had a deal in place, which was slightly different from our deal. Either way, in the end, you got what you wanted and I got what I wanted. I just hope that you were not in any way harmed during the process. If so, please accept my deepest apologies. I would tell you not to look for me, but I know that will not be the case. Sadly, for both of us, you will never see me again. But I hope the search will be more rewarding than the discovery. I truly wish things had worked out differently between us.

Paul

In a few hours I will touch down in Europe. From there, I will vanish, never to see Mariana, or the US government's covert operations team, again.

# . . . NOW YOU DON'T

**Location:** *Somewhere in Spain*
**Time:** *Unknown*

So, here we are, at the end of our time together. This is where my story ends for you, but not for me—and certainly not for Yuri. My hunt for him will not be concluded until I find him and exact my revenge. Once I have made him suffer for what he did to me, I will set my sites on my next target: the sheik.

By the way, I am an expert marksman with both handguns and rifles. I could have easily shot that peacock—or wounded it—if I wanted.

I am taking the Alta Velocidad Española across Spain, from Madrid to Seville in business class. I learned from a trusted source that Yuri might be visiting one of his many girlfriends there, a flamenco dancer named Olivia who is giving a performance this week.

As for Mariana, I never heard back from her. She might still be in Rodrigo's custody, or she might be back in Brazil, suffering through her marriage to Joe Sparty. Maybe she's divorced now and out of the government. I am laughing just thinking of the idea of someday reconnecting with her. For two people living in a world so different from ordinary men and women, the idea is ludicrous—but still intriguing. Even more so is that most people have no idea that the world I inhabit even exists. Ignorance is not bliss—it is just ignorant.

\* \* \*

This is my life. I am a consultant to some of the world's worst actors.

My name is Paul . . . or is it Marcus? Perhaps Noah, or Abraham?

I won't tell you because I don't know you, which means I don't trust you. And don't try to find out. If you—or my former American friends —try, for example, to find the transcripts of a Paul Ward who graduated from the University of Michigan Law School, there will be little to no record of him. A little further digging will reveal that a Paul Ward died in a car crash two weeks after his graduation, nearly twenty years ago. I assumed his identity as a precautionary measure, just in case I was ever detained by the authorities. I had rehearsed everything I told my handlers, continually in private for the past decade.

I confess that I have lied to you about many of the names, dates, and locations of my exploits. Did you really think that I would allow you enough clues to piece together my true identity? I'm not six feet four inches tall; that's too specific information. Hell, I don't even quote Sun Tzu. Rather, I prefer the teachings of Thucydides from his book, *The Peloponnesian War*. It's been said that General Colin Powell kept the following quote from Thucydides on his desk throughout his military and diplomatic career: "*Of all manifestations of power, restraint impresses men most.*"

You see, anonymity is my most valuable—and marketable— asset.

Who knows, you may have had a conversation with me in an airport. Or, I could be sitting next to you right now. But if you want to know what I've been up to, just to turn on the television, log onto the internet, or pick up a newspaper. Search the headlines of what is going on with a king, sheik, warlord, or dictator, and you might start reading about the results of my handiwork.

Such is my life as a clandestine consultant and this is where I leave you.

# ACKNOWLEDGMENTS

My sincerest thanks to all clandestine consultants who shared their stories with me and continue to shape world events . . . you know who you are, even though I may not know your true identities.

CPSIA information can be obtained
at www.ICGtesting.com
Printed in the USA
FFOW03n0320060118
44378920-44097FF